DON'T YOU TRUST ME?

Also by Patrice Kindl

Owl in Love

Goose Chase

Keeping the Castle

A School for Brides

PATRICE KINDL

DON'T

YOU

TRUST

ME?

 atheneum New York London Toronto Sydney New Delhi

atheneum

An imprint of Simon & Schuster Children's Publishing Division
1230 Avenue of the Americas, New York, New York 10020

For information about special discounts for bulk purchases, please contact Simon & Schuster Special Sales at 1-866-506-1949 or business@simonandschuster.com.
The Simon & Schuster Speakers Bureau can bring authors to your live event. For more information or to book an event, contact the Simon & Schuster Speakers Bureau at 1-866-248-3049 or visit our website at www.simonspeakers.com.
Also available in an Atheneum hardcover edition
Book design by Debra Sfetsios-Conover and Irene Metaxatos
The text for this book was set in Minion Pro.
Manufactured in the United States of America
First Atheneum paperback edition September 2017
10 9 8 7 6 5 4 3 2 1
The Library of Congress has cataloged the hardcover edition as follows:
Names: Kindl, Patrice, author.
Title: Don't you trust me? / Patrice Kindl.
Description: First edition. | New York : Atheneum Books for Young Readers, [2016] | Summary: Fifteen-year-old Morgan, an emotionless schemer, moves in with a family after impersonating their niece and will continue the deception no matter the cost.
Identifiers: LCCN 2015025075
ISBN 978-1-4814-5910-5 (hc)
ISBN 978-1-4814-5911-2 (pbk)
ISBN 978-1-4814-5912-9 (eBook)
Subjects: | CYAC: Impersonation—Fiction. | Deception—Fiction. | Conduct of life—Fiction. Classification: LCC PZ7.K5665 Do 2016 | DDC [Fic]—dc23
LC record available at http://lccn.loc.gov/2015025075

To Paul, who listened

DON'T YOU TRUST ME?

BELIEVE ME; I NEVER EXPECTED THINGS TO end up the way they did. But now that they *have*, I can't get all bent out of shape about it. I guess I figure I'm pretty much indestructible—I'm like one of those Super Balls: the harder you throw me, the higher I bounce.

See, I don't scare easily. I always assume I can get away with almost anything, so I do things on impulse that other people wouldn't do for fear of getting caught. And half the time I get away with some pretty outrageous stuff.

But then, of course, there's the other half of the time, when they find out. Then everybody has sixteen hissy fits and acts all *shocked* and *appalled*.

Still, I have no regrets. I don't waste my time on regrets. What I *do* try to do is learn from my mistakes. Not being afraid is great; it frees you up a lot. I can't even imagine how boring it must be to live like regular people, scared all the time. But living without fear *can* make your life harder. If you assume you are untouchable, you can find yourself taking stupid risks. And I am not stupid.

I learned about risk-taking when I was a little kid. Back then I had no idea that there were others like me in the world; I thought I was the only one. To be honest, the whole thing seemed kind of a joke. It was funny, watching people's faces change as it dawned on them how different I was.

I'm fifteen now, but it was meeting the carnival guy the summer when I was eight years old that got me to thinking about being different, and about what it meant for my future.

As usual my parents were punishing me for something or other, so they'd locked me in my room. There was this strawberry festival—nothing much, just crafts and face painting and strawberry shortcake with whipped cream. It's not like I even wanted to go, but since they said I couldn't, I climbed out my window that night and rode my bike downtown. I didn't have any money to buy anything, so I sat and watched this man who had a game booth set up next to the fried dough station. Something about him caught at my attention, the way a ragged fingernail or a loose tooth will nag at you. Finally I figured out what it was.

He was a cheat. He didn't cheat all the time. Every once in a while he let somebody win a lousy little stuffed animal, but mostly he cheated. His booth was low to the ground, so it was hard for adults to play, with kiddie stuff like dolls and robots and stuffed pink animals for prizes, and the game looked laughably easy. You had to throw a ball and knock down a bottle that was about two feet away, and then you won a prize. Only, somehow nobody ever did win, except if some grown-up got suspicious and insisted on trying it. *They* usually won some cheap thing, but kids never won anything.

He saw me watching him, but he didn't care. At one point this little kid with a twenty-dollar bill sticking out of his back pocket came and stood near the guy, looking on as his sister tried to win a pink unicorn. The guy reached around casually and tweaked the bill out of the kid's pocket. Then he winked at me.

I waited until both the boy and the girl had failed to win the unicorn and had gone away. I walked over to the guy.

"Care to try for a stuffed animal, little lady? It's easy! Every player a winner!"

I shook my head. "What've you got against kids?" I asked. "You never let anybody but grown-ups win."

"I got nothing against kids," he said. "They're my livelihood. They're stupid, see? They're easy to fool.

Grown-ups are more suspicious—they've gotten burned once or twice, maybe. I work these little community affairs instead of the big carnivals because they don't watch you so close." He sat back in his folding chair, studying me. "'Cause once they start asking questions and taking my game apart to see how it works, they'll shut me down. So every once in a while I got to let a grown-up win."

It ticked me off, the way he didn't care about me knowing he was crooked. "I could go tell those kids about that twenty you stole from them just now," I said. The expression on his face didn't change. He just sat there, looking at me.

"Or the cops," I added, jabbing at him a little harder. "I could tell the cops. *That* would get you shut down."

"Go ahead and try," he said, leaning forward to fluff out the skirt of a big princess doll so that it covered up the cheap teddy bears. "But I'll bet the cops already know you. Bet a pretty little girl like you already has a record with the local police. Don't you?"

I was silent a moment, and he went on, "Sure you do. I spotted you a mile off. You're one of *us*. You've got that stare."

That's when he told me about the cold people—the cold, he called them. He said there were lots of us—oh, not anywhere near as many as regular people, but maybe one in a hundred. "You got to learn how to spot them, but they're all over the place," he said. "You get so as you can recognize one of your own. Not that we *like* each other any more than we like anybody else, mind. So after we've had this talk, you can scram."

"Why 'the *cold*'?" I wanted to know.

"'Cause we're cold-blooded, like lizards. We don't love and we don't get scared. Bet you're here alone in the dark, without your family. Ain't you scared? Most little girls would be."

I thought over this information in silence for a while. "I don't have a *record*," I said. "Not a *police* record."

"Maybe not, but they know who you are, don't they?" he said. "There've been complaints, haven't there? Yeah, uh-huh." He nodded. "I thought so. Now beat it. I got lambs to fleece."

I beat it.

Riding home that night, I thought about what the carnie guy had said, and from then on I began to do things differently. Before, I'd have gone home whenever I felt like it. If my parents had been asleep, I'd have rung the doorbell over and over again until they'd gotten up and let me in. Then I'd have gone to my room and shut the door against their threats and pleas. It drove them crazy that I didn't care what they thought. Actually, I kind of enjoyed winding them up.

But this time I slid back through my bedroom window without making a noise. Maybe it wasn't as much fun, but it avoided trouble. Lately it had been like they expected me to be doing something wrong all the time, so they watched me pretty closely. If, like the carnie guy, I could lull them into a false sense of security, they might let up on the twenty-four-hour surveillance.

And, do you know, it worked?

After about a month of me doing mostly what I wanted to do, but hiding it, they relaxed. They started complimenting me on being so well behaved. They exchanged relieved smiles over my head as I pretended not to notice. And in a year it was like they had almost forgotten I was ever such a wild little thing.

Yeah, sure, it was more effort, but I got a whole lot more freedom.

I learned. And this kind of learning, as I later discovered, comes hard for people like us. Oh, we're smart enough—we can understand difficult concepts and master complex formulae. But when it comes to getting what we want, it is our tendency to just go for it.

The key is: the clever cold person learns self-control, learns to work around the ordinary people, in order to get what she wants in the long run. And the truth is, *that's* kind of fun, figuring out how to cover up my trail and put the normals on the wrong scent.

So, you ask, if I'm so smart, and I've learned to keep my true nature a secret, why am I telling *you* this?

I don't care if *you* know, because you will think that

I am *made up*. You will think I am *fictional*. And if you should happen to meet me in real life, you will never, ever guess.

But enough about you. Let's go on talking about me.

As I was saying, I got smart. In addition to obscuring my more questionable activities from my folks, I started keeping tabs on *them*. Three years ago, when I was twelve, I bugged their bedroom. You'd be amazed at the equipment you can buy online, and it's not that expensive either. Kind of gross, some of the stuff I heard as a result, but well worth it for the nuggets I picked up, things they would say to each other but never in front of me. I can't tell you how often that bug has saved my neck.

For instance, one time I was listening to my mother and father talking after I'd gone to my room. "Mrs. Pinckney from down the street called," my mom said. "She was asking if we knew anything about her cell phone. She says she left it on the front porch for half an hour, and when she went back, it was gone."

"Why would we have any idea what the Pinckney woman did with her cell phone?" my father said, sounding annoyed.

"Oh . . . I don't know . . . but maybe you could ask Morgan? [*I* am Morgan.] She does walk right past there on her way to the school bus."

"Why can't *you* ask her?"

"Oh, sweetheart, I'm sorry. She seems to take it much better coming from you. You know how I hate confronting her," my mother said, her voice getting high and panicky the way it does when she's stressed. "Please?"

"I really do not see why everyone in this neighborhood expects us to know the precise location of any valuables they happen to have misplaced, and I don't—"

I didn't hear the end of my father's complaint, because I was busy getting Mrs. Pinckney's cell out of my top dresser drawer. It was a cheap knockoff phone anyway, and I didn't care that I couldn't keep it. I know you can get credit card numbers and stuff off phones, but I had a feeling that if major purchases began showing up on her account, the finger of blame would start pointing in my direction pretty quickly. That woman has serious trust issues.

Anyway, I wasn't tempted by anything as blatant as credit card fraud. It's too easy to get caught, unless you live in Nigeria or someplace far, far away. No, I could have kicked myself for taking it, but the stupid woman had left it sitting out there in plain sight. What did she expect? You don't see *me* leaving things I care about lying around where somebody could lift them. Truth is, I'd taught her a valuable lesson about taking care of her possessions.

Still, I shouldn't allow my acquisitive instincts to overcome my better judgment. It's a fault, little though

I enjoy admitting to any shortcomings, and I intend to get the better of it. I let myself noiselessly in through the back door of Mrs. Pinckney's house. (Even after having her cell stolen, she *still* didn't lock the gate to her yard *or* her back door.) I could hear her yakking away on the house phone upstairs, to her married daughter this time. I found her gardening jacket hanging on a hook, a ratty old thing she only wore when she worked outdoors, and slipped the phone into a pocket. She'd find it soon enough.

As I closed the door behind me and walked back down the driveway to the street, I realized I ought to shape up and forget about that nickel-and-dime stuff. I needed to focus on long-term goals. I have plans for my future; I am going to go to law school, and then on to a career in the corporate world or politics, or both. I'm going to have a nice house in a much nicer neighborhood than ours, and I'll be highly respected by my neighbors and colleagues.

In fact, I'm going to do much, much better for myself than the usual cold one. Since that time at the strawberry festival so many years ago, I've encountered a number of others of my tribe, which isn't surprising. If you figure that the average high school has, like, a thousand students, that means that most schools would have enough of us enrolled to organize an after-school club. And when you consider that there's probably at least *one* .

of our kind on the staff, we could even have a faculty adviser.

Nah, I'm just teasing you. None of us would want to be out in the open like that, or to associate with others like ourselves. What did that old comedian say? "I refuse to join any club that'd have me as a member." Well, I mean, *duh*! You can't trust any of us as far as you can throw us. What kind of a club would that be?

But the point is, people like me are out there, if you know where to look. In fact, some of them are glaringly obvious. Boys, mostly, getting in major trouble with the law because they don't *think*. The girls are harder to spot; all that testosterone makes the boys act out in crazy ways, while the girls can learn to fly under the radar better.

I don't have much to do with them. Like I said, there's no percentage in getting friendly with other people like me—there's nothing to gain. We take; we don't give. Twenty years from now I'll be rich and respected. Who needs friends like that when you're in the A-list crowd?

Still, if that vision for me is going to come true, I have to be more careful, and stop doing idiotic things like stealing that cell phone just because it was sitting there unguarded.

And do you know what my parents did, after all my efforts to spare them grief? They decided to *send me away to boarding school*. They said it was because my mother was sick, which maybe she was. She'd been acting weird lately. To tell the truth, I think she's smarter than my dad. The way she looks at me sometimes . . . I know I make her nervous.

I wouldn't mind so much, only I looked at the brochure for the school, and buried under a lot of verbiage about "a challenging academic and athletic environment" was something about how it's appropriate for "troubled teens." I am *not* a troubled teen. I am entirely untroubled. I get good grades; I even have a few "friends."

How was I supposed to prepare for entrance into an elite college from a reform school? No way was I going to have that on my record.

But my parents were implacable. At least, my dad was. My mom just cried all the time. Anytime I tried to talk to her, she burst into tears and rushed to her room. I tried playing the guilt card. I accused them of not loving me, of thinking I'm not good enough to live up to their expectations. Dad wouldn't budge. Mom cried.

One night my father came into my room and packed a suitcase for me.

"We're headed for the airport by seven a.m., so you'd better set your alarm. A representative of the New Beginnings School will be waiting for you at the Phoenix airport. I'm sorry, Morgan, but my decision on this is final."

"What did I do?"

"Nothing," he said, avoiding my eyes. "Nothing at all.

11

But your mother needs a rest. And so do I. It is for your own good. Be ready to go by seven."

Oh well. This place was kind of played out for me, anyway. Maybe it was time for me to head out, try for a fresh start.

2

MY FATHER DIDN'T STAY TO SEE ME OFF AT THE airport. He lectured me all the way there on how I was to behave myself at school, and then dropped me in front of the terminal. He hauled my suitcase out of the trunk, gave me a hasty peck on the cheek, and jumped back into the car, hitting the button that made the locks *thunk* down. He realized what he had done—locked me out in case I tried to stage a last-minute return—and raised guilty eyes to meet mine in the rearview mirror. As he drove away, he hunched over the wheel and put his foot to the accelerator like all the hounds of Hades were in pursuit.

Really, I had to laugh.

Anyway, I didn't go through security right away

because it was hours before my flight. Once you're through the TSA screening, they coop you up in the gate area and won't let you out. It makes me crazy being fenced in and told I can't go where I want. So there I was, kicking back in the lounge, bored and ticked off and looking around for some kind of diversion. The place was packed, with groups of people camped out on the floor. The only seat I could find was next to a wet mess of a girl who was about my own age.

Sob, sob, sob. I mean, I'm a blonde too, and when you're a blonde with that thin, pale skin that goes all red and patchy under stress, you ought to know better than to cry in public. Or at all. Her whole face was swollen: eyes, nose, mouth, everything was bloated up like an overstuffed sausage. She was honking into a series of tissues that got wetter and snottier by the second. After a while the racket began to wear on me.

"What's the matter?" I asked, more to shut up the noise than because I cared. Her neighbors on the other side were studiously ignoring Weeping Wanda, so I was obviously the only one who was going to tackle the situation.

"Th-they're s-sending me a-a-*way!*" she hiccuped. "They don't want me to see him again, but I will, I swear I will!"

"*Who* is sending you away?" I asked patiently. "Who is *him*?"

The blonde paused in her lamentations long enough to stare at me like *I* was the crazy one.

"My *parents*, of course. They're sending me away to stay with my cousin so I can't see my *boyfriend* anymore. They *hate* him."

This struck a chord. "Yeah, my parents are sending me away too," I offered. "Not to relatives, but boarding school. Only it's because they don't like *me*, not because they don't like my boyfriend."

She lowered the soggy mass of tissues from her eyes. "Don't be silly," she said. "Your parents like you. They *have* to like you. You're their *child*. They're probably sending you away because they think it's for your own good. That's what mine keep telling me, anyway. Like they know what's good for me! If I don't get to see Ashton again I will die, and then how will they feel?" She returned to her tissues.

"Oh sure, that's what my parents say too," I agreed, "but the truth is, they're happier when I'm not around, and they're willing to pay for the privilege."

"That's *terrible*," she said, momentarily distracted from her own woes. Then she shook her head. "No, I'm sure you must be wrong. It's, like, a rule. Parents always love their children, even if they don't understand them. Which mine sure don't."

I shrugged, unwilling to argue the point. However, having spared a millisecond of her attention for my affairs, she had returned to her own. She pointed at a man who was walking away from us. *"There,"* she said in an accusing undertone. "That's my father. I'm waiting for him to hit the men's room before I go through the security line. He's hoping that before I leave I'll say that I forgive him and that I'm okay with being *kidnapped* to New York. But I'm not. I hate him."

I nodded, unmoved by her predicament.

"I'd give anything, *anything*, if only I could get away and go live with Ashton," she said, her voice wailing monotonously up and down like a bagpipes player practicing scales. "He doesn't know I'm leaving, and they took my *phone* away from me so I can't talk to him. They wouldn't even *let me say good-bye to him.*"

"So, why don't you leave?" I asked. "When you get to your cousin's, you could call him, couldn't you? Then you could take a bus back, or he could come get you."

"No!" She was getting petulant. "Because if I ran away, they'd know it. My aunt and uncle would call my parents, and they'd start searching for me. I'm only sixteen. We wouldn't be allowed to get married or anything. My dad is standing over me like a creepy old vulture, ready to watch me walk onto that plane. And then my aunt is waiting like another vulture at the other end to grab me the second I walk off the plane. *There is no escape.*"

"Uh-huh," I said. This female was beginning to bore

me. My eyes strayed across the crowded room, looking for another empty seat. There wasn't one.

So, suck it up, Blondie, I thought. A hot, damp hand closed on my wrist.

"It's *HIM*!"

"Him who?"

"*Him*! Ashton! Oh, isn't he the most beautiful guy you've ever seen?"

I looked where she was looking, my eyes narrowing. Leather jacket, curly hair, short, muscular body. Definitely several years older than his girlfriend—in his twenties, I'd say. I could see why Mom and Dad wanted to ship Blondie out of state. The guy was definitely hot. Truth was, she didn't deserve him.

"Not bad," I conceded. "You're a little young for him, aren't you? I'm surprised your parents don't just sic the cops on him."

"They're *threatening* to! That's the only reason I agreed to go away. But now he's found out I'm leaving, and he's come for me! I'll never get away with my dad here. You have to help me! You have to!" She was still hanging on to my wrist, half looking imploringly at me, half looking at Ashton.

I was looking at her hand on my wrist, about to pry her fingers off one by one, but all the same, my mind had begun to churn. Was there something in this for me? "What do you want me to do?"

"I don't know! You seem really smart. I know you can help me. Oh, Ashton! He doesn't see me!"

"Stop waving at him," I snapped, irritated. "Don't try to attract his attention or call him over here, you dope, or your father will come out of the men's room and see him. I'll go talk to him and get him to lay low. Don't let anybody else sit in my seat, including your father. Now *get your hands off me.*"

Reluctantly she let go. I rose and went to talk to Ashton, who was scanning the crowded room, looking in exactly the wrong direction. He was cute, all right, but possibly not very smart.

"Hey," I said when I got close. "Don't look now, but your girlfriend is behind you, about a hundred feet—Hey! I said, *don't look*! Her father's here somewhere too."

"Who're you?" He was chewing gum with his mouth open, looking me over.

"A friend. A friend who's going to fix everything so that you two lovebirds can be together. Only, are you sure you want her? 'Cause she seems like more trouble than she's worth."

He went on chewing, giving himself a long moment to think this through. "You mean Janelle? Sure I want her. We're in love."

"Okay, fine, just checking," I said. Yeah, he was dumb. Too bad. Still, nobody could say I didn't give him a chance to back out. "Here, c'mon over where we can talk without your future father-in-law seeing us." I motioned him behind a big cement pillar. "Sit down here. Don't move," I said, speaking in short, easy-to-understand sentences. "Wait until Janelle comes for you. We're going to convince Janelle's father that she got on the plane. After he leaves, you and Janelle can too."

He chewed his gum for a while longer. "Okay, I guess. Tell Janelle we can go stay at my uncle's fishing cabin in the mountains. It's on a little lake and it's real pretty this time of year. My uncle doesn't go there after the last week of July."

"Fine," I said. "But remember! Sit quietly here until Janelle comes up to you. That's when it'll be safe to show yourself. And it could be a while, so be patient."

"Uh-huh." He sat down obediently, and I wound my way back through the crowd to Janelle.

"Oh, did you talk to him? What did he say? Is he upset?"

"Seemed okay to me," I said. "You and he are going to have a honeymoon at his uncle's fishing cabin if I can manage it."

"Oh, how romant—"

"Keep your voice down. When does your flight leave?"

The tears welled up again. "In forty minutes! I have to go through security any second. Oh! Here comes my dad!"

"Fine. Excellent. Go tell your father you're going to the ladies' room and you'll meet him at security when they call the flight."

"Oh, but . . . shouldn't I be on the way through security now?"

"Not if you want to catch fish with Ashton, you shouldn't. You have to wait until the last minute. Your father wouldn't go looking for you in the ladies' room, would he? Or at least not until he thought you were about to miss the flight?"

She giggled a little. "Not even then," she said. "My dad is kind of a prude."

"Okay, then. We're in business. Go tell him. Then get to the restroom over there in the far corner. I'll be inside."

"But—there's a closer one, nearer to the security checkpoint."

"Exactly. You are not going to that one, but if you want to suggest to your dad that you *are*, like by pointing in that direction, that'd be fine. He'll be expecting you to be coming from there instead of from way back *there*, see?"

Janelle looked bewildered.

"Just do it. Point at the ladies' room near the checkpoint, and then kind of sidle around back to the other one. I'll be waiting for you there." I got up and left. Either she'd do it or she wouldn't. I'd wait for ten minutes.

The ladies' room was crowded, but there was a bench near the mirror and I sat down.

Two minutes later she pushed through the door. "Oh, he's so mad! He wanted me to go through security, like, immediately. He said I could use the ladies' room in the gate area or on the plane. I said I had to go really, really—"

"Good. Now get into a stall and take off your clothes down to your underwear."

"*What?*"

"We're going to change clothes, dummy. I'll take your place on the plane, and you wait here until the flight has taken off and your father has gone home. Then you go find Ashton, see?"

"But—"

"But nothing. It'll work. We're the same height. We're both blondes. You've got a scarf around your neck that I'll wear on my head. I'm going to come running out of here at the last minute, wave to your father, and disappear into the security zone. Got it?"

"Oh, but . . . but what about when you get there, when you get to Albany? My aunt and uncle will be waiting for me."

"When's the last time you saw them?"

She wrinkled up her face, thinking. "Um . . . I think when I was about seven? Yeah. We went to stay with them for a week one summer. It's kind of outside of a small city—not like Los Angeles."

"Perfect. You've changed since you were seven."

She looked at me critically. "Your eyes are a deeper blue than mine," she said.

"Contact lenses," I said.

"You weigh maybe fifteen pounds less than I do. I'm curvier."

"So I've been on a diet." Actually, it was more like twenty-five pounds.

"My mom might have sent photographs—"

"Look, none of this is a problem. I'll disappear as soon as I get there. They'll never see me and I won't see them. Go on, get in there and start handing over your clothes. When I'm not waiting for them at the airport, and they do start looking for you, they'll see by the passenger list that you traveled on that flight but slipped away before they spotted you. So they'll be looking from there, not LA, see?"

"Yeah," she said slowly. "I guess so."

In the end we got adjoining toilet stalls, so it was easy to hand blouses and jeans under the partition wall. Eventually we emerged and looked at each other. We laughed.

"Not *too* bad," I said.

"I guess," she said. "We *are* a lot alike."

"It'll work from a distance, anyway," I said. "I just can't let your father see me up close, that's all."

She opened her mouth to wail about something or other, but the announcer came on, talking about her flight. She gasped. "Go! They're calling my plane!"

"Oh, for crying out loud," I said. "This is the first time they've announced it. We're waiting until the last minute, remember?"

"Oh yeah. Okay."

"I need your ticket. Oh, and some identification."

Janelle fished the ticket out of her purse. This she handed over without hesitation but was less happy about the ID.

"My learner's permit!" she mourned. "I waited so long to get it!"

"You'll have to assume a new identity anyway," I pointed out. "You couldn't have used it."

"Yeah, well. I guess."

"What do you call your father? Dad? Daddy? Popsie?"

"Dad, of course. Are you going now?"

"In ten minutes."

"Ten minutes! You'll miss it!"

"No I won't. I run fast." I sat down and pulled out a magazine from my carry-on luggage. As I leafed through it, Janelle fidgeted. I could tell she was mentally pushing me out the bathroom door, whispering *Go! Go!* in her head.

A woman came in and laid a squalling baby on the changing table. She cooed at the kid in an unsuccessful attempt to make it stop shrieking while she wiped its dirty butt. I turned a menacing stare onto the infant, and it hushed abruptly. You'd think the woman would have been grateful, but she got huffy, bundled the kid back up, and left, shooting resentful looks in my direction.

Janelle kept checking her watch and sighing.

At last I got up and said, "Well, it's been nice knowing you. Better hang on for another half hour in here. For all you know, your dad might wait to see the plane actually leave." Not that I particularly cared about Janelle and Ashton's future, but I didn't want Janelle's family calling ahead to have me detained as I walked off the plane. I was hoping we could pull this off so I'd have some breathing room for a few days until I decided what to do next.

I held the ticket and learner's permit in one hand and my carry-on in the other—I realized that I was going to lose my big suitcase, checked in for Phoenix—and shot out of the ladies' room, plowing into a bevy of flight attendants.

"Gangway! Coming through," I yelled. I scanned the area for Janelle's father. Yep, there he was, looking anxiously at his watch and peering nervously in through the door of the other ladies' room. I bellowed "Dad! I've got to run," waved frantically—taking care to keep my threshing hand in front of my face—and bolted past him, pounding through the rope line in front of security. I thrust my ticket and ID at the agent, gasping, "I'm gonna miss it! Please hurry!"

She took one quick look at the photo, one quick, irritated look at me, and then processed the ticket.

"Better not cut it so close next time, young lady," she called after me as I raced toward the scanner machines. The flight attendant looked pretty annoyed as I flung myself in through the door to the airplane, but she helped me to my seat and stowed my carry-on for me.

Almost immediately after I sat down the door shut and the engines started humming. The plane slowly eased out of its position against the gate and began to taxi toward the runway.

And off I went.

3

"ARE YOU JANELLE? WELL, YOU MUST BE. YOU look exactly like your picture. And of course I'm your cousin Brooke. It's been so long since we've seen each other; I bet I look totally different from what you remember, right?"

"Sure," I said. She was another blue-eyed blonde like me and Janelle, on the plump side. And as dim as her cousin, if she thought I looked *exactly* like a picture of Janelle. No aunt or uncle in sight, so I guess she got sent alone to pick me up at the airport.

Why was I even talking to her, you ask? Yeah, I know I said I'd disappear once I got to Albany, but I changed my mind. So sue me.

"Sorry I'm late," she prattled on, "but the traffic was

awful. Don't we need to go to the baggage claim to get your luggage?" she asked, tagging along like a little duckling as I rode down the escalator. I shook my head and held up my carry-on bag. "You mean that little thing is all you've got? Well, I'm glad you're not one of those girls who needs to travel with a whole shopping mall full of clothing changes and makeup. Still, I don't think I could move across the country for a whole two years with only one little carry-on. If you want, we can go shopping before school starts. I already got my fall wardrobe, but if you need to get some things, I'll be happy to do it over again with you."

I opened my mouth to respond but was forestalled.

"I'm crazy about airports, aren't you?" my newfound cousin asked, gazing around, wide-eyed, as she chattered. "There're always good-looking boys at the airport. And I love watching the people, especially families who've been separated. Military families, you know? The mom or the dad has been overseas in danger—they could have died, or come home missing a leg or something—and the spouse and the kids are so excited and so relieved to see them alive and okay. They're really happy to see each other. It makes you feel better about humanity, I always think. Oh, look at that little girl—how sweet! Isn't she darling?"

I looked where she was pointing, at a particularly foul specimen of beribboned and beruffled toddlerhood, who seemed to be having a meltdown in the lounge area.

"Mmm," I said, and followed the Babbling Brooke out into the August heat.

"Right this way. This is the parking garage. Well, of course." She giggled. "What else would it be? An ugly hotel, I guess. This airport is pretty small, probably, after what you're used to. I always park kind of far back because I'm afraid my car will get scratched. Aggressive drivers tend to park up front, that's what they say." She sucked in some oxygen to fuel the next gush of words as we approached a little green convertible.

"It's a Miata roadster. My car, I mean. I've wanted one my whole life ever since I saw one as, like, a baby. I saved up my money for years and years, but of course my father paid for most of it. It was used, but it's in perfect condition. I wash and wax it every Saturday. Or Sunday, if it's raining or something on Saturday. There's a car wash just outside our neighborhood so it's easy even in bad weather. But if it's nice out, I like to do it in the driveway. Do you have your driver's license yet? No, you probably don't. You're six months younger than me, and lots of people take a couple of tries to pass."

I managed to insert four words into the stream of verbiage: "I have my permit." Of course, I didn't actually have *my* permit, but I had Janelle's, so what's the difference?

"Oh great, but probably you won't be able to drive my

car because it's a stick shift. It's not like I wouldn't let you if you could drive stick shift, but you can't, can you?" Here she actually paused for my response.

"No," I admitted.

"Oh good. Well, not 'good,' of course. But I admit I was a little teeny bit worried. Because I love my car so much. I'm sure you understand."

"I'm an exceptionally good driver," I said. This was not quite true. My parents flatly refused to let me touch the steering wheel of their little tin-can car until I had a permit (and they kept the keys under close supervision), so I had zero driving experience. But I figured that possession of Janelle's permit entitled me to claim her experience. Why shouldn't she be a good driver? "I could learn to drive stick shift," I added, regarding the little car with interest. "I'll bet this baby can go really fast."

"Oh! Well . . . we'll see. Maybe you could try driving the SUV first. Actually, I drive *slower* in the Miata than I do in the SUV. It's so low to the ground, it makes you *feel* like you're going a lot faster."

"Seems like kind of a waste of a sports car, doesn't it? If it were mine, I'd want to push it to the limit, so I knew how much power it had."

Brooke fell silent for the first time in our twenty-minute acquaintance, no doubt seeing visions of crushed and mangled roadster before her eyes. I settled into the passenger seat as she lifted my carry-on into the trunk.

She didn't speak again until we were on the highway, zipping along with the wind in our hair and the sun on our faces. Oh yeah, I could get used to this form of transport. The most notable thing about the scenery whizzing past was that it was green: yellow green, moss green, blue green—more greens than in an L.L.Bean catalog. At home things are brown and olive, mostly. And the air felt different; kind of moist and balmy.

"Um, so, Janelle—"

"Morgan," I corrected absentmindedly, watching how she moved her feet on the pedals, trying to fathom the mysteries of driving stick.

"What?"

"Oh," I said, resurfacing. "Um, I mean, I've decided that I hate that name. It's so stupid-sounding." Which is nothing but the truth. *Janelle?* Give me a break. "I always wanted to be called 'Morgan,' so I figured this would be the right time to make the change, moving to a new place and all." My parents did give me one thing I liked: my name.

"Oh wow, really? 'Morgan'? It almost sounds like a guy's name."

"Sometimes it is," I said. "It's unisex." I like that about it. It sounds strong, a little tough. Like me.

"Well, okay . . . Morgan. Anyway, I hear your mom and dad are trying to break up your romance," she said.

"If you don't want to talk about it, that's fine, but if you do, I can sympathize. What happened?"

I considered this question for a long moment. If there is one thing I pride myself on, it's making up a good story. Oh, how tempting it was at that moment to open my mouth and see what came out! It would be a sad story, for sure, one that would get Brooke entirely on my side. An exciting story, one that would make those blue eyes bug out with amazement, a tale of thwarted lovers, cruel parents, unjust accusations, and violent deeds. If I could count on not staying long with Brooke's family, it didn't have to be entirely believable either. I sighed regretfully. It would have been great, but . . .

See, I'd had time to think on the plane ride. That's why, even though I *had* said I would disappear as soon as I got to Albany, I'd changed my plans.

I'd been so pleased by my own cleverness in switching places with Janelle that I hadn't thought much about the future. My old weakness, I admit. On a sudden impulse I will launch out over thin ice, improvising brilliantly, skating faster and faster until I've reached the other side of the pond. The problem was that this time the pond was more like an ocean and I could see some pretty big cracks forming under my feet.

I wasn't too worried about my own family figuring out where I was. The people at New Beginnings were bound to notice when I didn't show up, and they'd tell my parents. They'd check the passenger manifest and see I hadn't gotten on the plane. Knowing I didn't have the money for another plane ticket, everybody would assume I had taken off from the LA airport, hitchhiking or whatever. Nobody would guess in a million years where I was; I was safe from them at the moment.

But if I wasn't going to go to school at New Beginnings, where *was* I going to spend the next two or three years? And how was I going to go about getting into my elite college, with no high school transcript or fixed address to offer? And then there was money. I'm smart, all right, but my grades weren't of that stellar quality that provides a totally free ride at an upper-echelon school. My parents were irritatingly lower-middle-class. They didn't earn anywhere near enough to make paying tuition at a good school easy, but they did earn a bit too much to get me in on a needs-based scholarship. Frankly, they must have been desperate to get rid of me, to have forked over the money for New Beginnings.

Come to think of it, any money they might have saved for my college education would have gone down the drain of New Beginnings. They had nothing to offer me now, so no point in sticking around.

Oh well. I gave myself a vigorous mental shake, like a dog after a bath. I would worry about those details later. But for the moment I needed to tone down my natural flamboyance and tell a story these people would believe.

This was not the time to indulge in theatrics. I needed to hang on to the free room and board this family offered.

Still, I couldn't help but add a little spice. . . .

"It's not a nice story," I said. "My parents— Well, I'm sorry, but I don't know you well enough to go into the details. I mean, your mother and my father *are* brother and sister. I can't risk it."

"Oh. Um, you mean *your* mother and *my* father, don't you?"

"Yeah, okay, whatever. It's just, my father can get ugly. If he knew I'd told—"

"Oh! Wow, really? Uncle John? I never would have thought— But you know him better, of course—"

"Maybe later," I said, casting a somber look in her direction, signaling my willingness to divulge all sorts of sordid details, once we had gotten to know each other.

She nodded solemnly. "Whenever you feel you can talk about it, I'll be honored to listen. I'm only sorry I asked, when it's such a sensitive subject! Gee— Eek!" In her anxiety to express her contrition she hadn't been paying attention to her driving, and she swerved out of the way of an ice cream truck. "Golly, I'm *sorry!*"

Golly? I mean, I had long ago broken myself of the habit of swearing—it just draws unfavorable attention from people in authority and isn't worth the release it offers—but, "golly"? Who was she, Nancy Drew, girl detective?

As things developed, yeah, that's pretty much who she was. Her dad owned a chain of car dealerships—Brooke pointed one out as we drove by—and he clearly doted on his daughter. The mother was a nonentity. She had some kind of job outside the house, I guess, but she was so stupendously boring to talk to that I couldn't seem to concentrate on what she was saying for more than five minutes at a time, so I didn't catch what her job was, and anyway, of course they thought I already knew, so they didn't exactly spell it out.

They didn't spell out *any* of the things I needed to know. None of them, except Brooke, had the courtesy to introduce themselves, so I had to guess at their names. I mean, it was no help for Brooke to explain them away as "my mom and my dad." I kinda figured that's who the man and woman having drinks in the living room of her house must be. But *I* could hardly call them that, could I? In a pinch I supposed I could just say "Uncle" and "Aunt," but I was going to have to go through the trash looking for old envelopes if I didn't find out pretty soon.

The house was supernice. The car dealerships were apparently doing okay, or there was family money; *something* was funding this kind of lavishness. Looking around at the layout, I found myself nodding slowly and thinking, *Yes, there could have been much, much worse places to land.* Dumb ol' Janelle, to trade this in for a fishing cabin with Ashton!

The neighborhood I'd grown up in was nothing like this. One thing I noticed—hardly any chain-link fences. At home in LA every teeny little house had its teeny little yard surrounded with chain-link. Here, if there *were* any fences, they were decorative and cost serious money. Mostly the huge, green lawn from one house blended in with the huge, green lawn of the neighboring house. It was like they didn't even care if you treated their yard as a public park. Back where I come from, they'd kill you for *looking* at their stupid ten blades of grass.

On the other hand, at home you could get into the car and drive through neighborhoods where people were a hundred times richer than this, where movie stars and billionaires lived. Well, you could so long as they didn't live in gated communities, anyway. Around here, this was probably as rich as people got. In any case, it was a fancier place than I'd ever lived in.

I'd never known anybody with a swimming pool, indoor hot tub, *and* a sauna before, that's for sure. Big-screen televisions everywhere you looked, every bedroom with an attached bath, a *four*-car garage—and there were only three people in the household!

My bedroom was the size of the living room at home, and I could have swum a few laps in the bathtub. And, I know it's girly of me, but I've always *wanted* a canopied bed. There were golden tassels twined around the posts, and the duvet was printed with Early-American-type cherries. On the big walnut desk I found one of those computers that can be a laptop or a tablet. All for me!

Dinner was four courses, none of which appeared to have ever been near a microwave. The food had sauces and contrasting flavors and was arranged artfully on my plate. Could there have been a professional chef out there in the kitchen? At home we mostly had frozen pizza and Lean Cuisine.

Brooke's mom asked if I was feeling homesick.

"No, not at all," I said, forking up the last tiny bit of cheesecake with raspberries.

"Oh, well, I'm going to call your parents in a few minutes to let them know you arrived safely. I'm sure you'd like to talk to them."

"Nope. Thanks anyway," I said. I leaned back in my chair, lovingly digesting each dish of that memorable meal.

The adults exchanged looks.

"Janelle—I mean *Morgan* is still kind of mad at her parents," Brooke whispered.

"We understand . . . er, Morgan," said the dad. "I think we understand about your new name too. It's not a bad idea—a new name, a new life, a new identity. We're going to do everything we can to help you forget this past, difficult year, and in this new home you can create a whole new self that is stronger and happier in every way than the old one. Do you think you can work with us on that?"

I looked around the table at my new family—handsome, successful-looking dad, a little flushed with wine; anxious, dumpy mom; and blond, plump Brooke.

"Thanks," I said. I smiled at them, a wavering, thin, courageous smile. "Actually, yes, with your help, I think I can."

4

"OH, JA—ER, MORGAN, THE AIRLINES CALLED. They say they have your bag there." It was the following morning, and my new aunt (I was calling her Auntie X to myself) was pouring herself another cup of coffee before leaving for her whatever-it-was job, while I breakfasted on yogurt, granola, fresh fruit, and orange juice. *Hand-squeezed* orange juice!

Brooke looked up from her own meal and said, "Hey, I thought you said you only had that one carry-on bag."

Oops. Probably it was Janelle's luggage, checked through from LA with a phone number right on the tag, and those busybodies at the airport had to go and call me on it. I hadn't thought about that. Well, poop.

I'd been looking forward to the promised shopping expedition. When in doubt, spread the blame around, and lay most of it on somebody who's not actually in the room.

"The airline lost it," I lied. "I *did* try to tell you, but . . ." I trailed off and shot Auntie X a rueful little look.

Auntie X picked up her cue. "Brooke, *really*! I suppose the poor girl was trying to squeeze a few words in edgewise and you talked right over her. Why don't you two run back and pick it up after breakfast? You can take J—Morgan on a tour of the town, show her the school and so on."

I supposed I was going to have to get used to being called "J—Morgan," at least for a while.

"Okay," said Brooke slowly. "But we never even checked the luggage return carousel. How did you know they lost it?"

"The flight attendant told me," I said, taking another swallow of fresh-squeezed goodness. "Don't know how *she* knew," I added, forestalling any further inquiry. "I kind of thought it must have been rerouted to Timbuktu and that was the last I'd ever see of it." Thinking quickly, I added, "I wasn't that sorry, either. None of those clothes fit me very well anymore."

Brooke's eyes rounded. "Oh, you mean, like that shirt you were wearing yesterday? I *thought* it was a little baggy on you."

"Brooke!"

"Well, Mom, I'm just saying it looked like Morgan lost some weight recently."

"Personal remarks are *never* either wise or polite," Auntie X said sternly.

I bestowed a sunny smile on Auntie X and Brooke. "Oh, I don't mind! I think I look better this way." Janelle *was* a bit too voluptuous. In my opinion my more slender, toned body was much more attractive.

"Your mother didn't mention that you were on a diet," Auntie X said. "You don't need to lose any more, certainly."

My expression flipped from sunshine to gloom. "My mother didn't mention it because I *wasn't* on a diet. She knows perfectly well why I lost that weight. So naturally she didn't mention it."

"Oh?" she said. "Stress, you mean?" She eyed my plate, which had been all but licked clean. "Well, I'm glad to see that your appetite has picked up."

"Yeah, I feel a lot happier here," I said. "*Safer*, you know. Thanks for having me. And," I added as an afterthought, "of course *you* aren't doing that Tough Love thing with the food restrictions."

"*What?* Food restrictions?" Auntie X stared at me, blinking her pink rabbit eyes. "Jackie said nothing about— Insofar as I know, the Tough Love program does not advocate withholding food!"

I made my face crumple with dismay and covered my mouth with my hands. "Oh no! Oh, I am so sorry—I didn't mean to say that! I promised my parents— *Please* forget I ever said anything." I shook my head and made earnest eye contact. "It's not true. My parents didn't withhold food from me, honest they didn't."

Auntie X and Brooke looked at me doubtfully. Then they looked at each other. When their gazes shifted back to me again, there was concern and sympathy in their eyes.

"I *see*," said Auntie X.

"Gee *whiz*," said Brooke.

Wow. I was so good at this.

By the time Auntie X had departed for work and Brooke and I had cleared our plates (there *was* a cook in the kitchen, but "We try to help Mrs. Barnes out as much as we can," explained Little Miss Goody Two-Shoes Brooke), I was beginning to believe my own story. I could almost remember the dreadful weeks before I was sent away, locked in my room on a steady diet of water and Wheat Thins. Who could blame me for not wanting to see or speak to parents who would do an awful thing like that? Would it be possible to spin out these cushy lodgings for my final two years of high school with no one the wiser? Then Janelle's parents would be the ones coughing up the money for my college tuition, instead of my semi-impoverished real parents. Serve them right too, the child abusers!

I found myself sincerely hoping that Janelle and Ashton would find true happiness together. Because if she went running home to Mommy and Daddy, everybody might subsequently get to wondering who *I* was.

I had great faith in my ability to improvise on the spur of the moment, but trying to explain the existence of two Janelles, one on each side of the continent, might be hard even for me. However, no need to fuss over it now. My immediate future was rosy.

It had clouded up and looked like rain, so Brooke didn't want the top down. Irritating, as with the top up the ride wasn't half as much fun. I pointed out a number of patches of blue overhead, but the stubborn girl refused to reconsider, claiming that rain would damage her leather upholstery.

She wasn't quite as chatty as she had been yesterday on the way back from the airport. She seemed to be thinking. I didn't mind. I sat and watched the scenery go by.

"I heard your mom and dad confiscated your cell phone," she said at last. "That must be awful. I can't imagine living without my phone."

I opened my mouth to ask her what she was talking about, and then realized that yeah, Janelle's parents probably had taken her cell away to keep her from contacting Ashton—in fact, she'd even told me so. It was therefore going to be necessary to hide my own miserable little phone—the cheapest model my tightfisted parents could find.

I thought about this. *Actually, I probably should get rid of it.* Couldn't they track your location through your cell, even if it didn't have a GPS? New Beginnings had for sure already informed my family that I hadn't arrived, and they'd know by now that my plane ticket hadn't been used. I wanted them to think I had left LAX on foot or by car and was therefore still in California. If my cell showed that I was suddenly in New York . . .

"I suppose I could get one of those pay-as-you-go phones," I said. "You know, like, from Walmart?"

"You could," admitted Brooke. "I—I won't mention it to my parents, if you'd rather I didn't," she offered. I had to stifle a laugh; that was a generous offer from a prissy-pants like Brooke.

"Only," she said, darting a little look at me, "maybe it would be better if you didn't call your boyfriend, since your parents don't want you to?"

"I wasn't planning to call Ashton," I said, which was a fact, since I didn't know his number. "If I did, what would we talk about? Weep on each other's shoulders because we can't be together? Somehow . . . he and the rest of my friends seem like strangers to me." Again, I was speaking nothing but the truth. "In fact," I mused aloud, "who would I call if I had a phone? Nobody. What's the point? I guess I won't bother." I heaved a leaden sigh and stared out at the horizon.

"Morgan, I'm so sorry. You *are* having a tough year. I wish there was something I could do to cheer you up," said Brooke.

"We-e-e-l-l," I said, "you *could* put the top down. And if it *did* start to rain, I could put it up again at a red light."

"Oh, Morgan," she said with a laugh.

But she pulled over the next chance she got, and we put the top down. The sun came out from behind the clouds and the wind whipped through our hair, and everybody we passed stared after us enviously.

Yeah, I could get used to this life. . . .

Janelle's clothes were definitely too big on me, especially in the bust. However, they were a lot more expensive than the ones I used to wear, so I spent some time in my room trying them on and seeing which ones could be adapted for my figure. There were lots of things, like scarves and jewelry and even shoes, that I could use, and I enjoyed my exploration of the suitcase. Janelle would be getting pretty sick of wearing the same outfit soon, though maybe you didn't need too many clothes on your honeymoon.

Tap, tap, tap! It was Brooke knocking on my bedroom door.

"Um . . . Morgan, there's something funny. . . . Could you come and look at this?"

Obediently I followed her into her room. Hmm. Definitely bigger than mine, and crammed with goodies. Brooke's laptop was showing a Facebook feed page. Her finger pointed out a post. I sat down at her desk and looked at it.

That stupid Janelle!

She was supposed to be incommunicado in the wilderness, lying low in order to evade detection, yet here she was on Facebook, posting a GIF animation of herself embracing Ashton in front of a muddy-looking body of water. Over and over and over again she bent to kiss him, in a never-ending loop.

I uttered a hiss of fury. Brooke looked at me, wide-eyed.

"Who is that?" she asked. "Somebody is posting under your name. It's your account—remember? We became Facebook friends a week before you came." She studied the image for a moment. "She kind of looks like you."

"She does not," I said coldly, eying the little roll of fat on Janelle's stomach. "She's got to be thirty pounds heavier than I am, and trust me, that hair is dyed."

"But who *is* she?"

"Mary Ellen Lipinski," I said, conjuring this name up out of nowhere. "My *ex-friend*. And that"—I pointed an accusing finger at Ashton's self-satisfied face—"is my *ex-boyfriend*. How *could* they? I haven't even been gone for twenty-four hours."

"Oh, Morgan!" cried Brooke, aghast. "I am so sorry! That's terrible!" She reached out her hand and touched my arm gently. "But," she said, her face clouding over with confusion, "why would she post using your name?"

"You don't know the half of it," I said, my voice somber. *I* didn't know the half of it. I opened my mouth and waited to hear what would come out of it. What villainy could Mary Ellen Lipinski be guilty of?

"I didn't want to believe she would go this far, but I guess it's only logical if you think about it." I stared at the jerky image of the couple, who appeared to be trying to eat each other's faces. "She has been . . . How do I explain? Ever since she transferred to our school last year, she's been trying to *turn into* me. She's copied my hair style—she even dyed it to match my color. She bought the same clothes and made her voice sound like mine. And since I've left town, she's taken over my boyfriend and my Facebook identity! I don't believe it!"

"Wow," said Brooke. She shook her head slowly. "Wow."

"*That's* why I changed my name," I added, inspired. "I didn't realize exactly what she was doing, but it was beginning to give me the creeps. People had started saying we looked like twins."

"What about Ashton?" Brooke inquired gently. "He's part of this too. I mean"—she gestured at his grinning face—"it doesn't look like she's holding a gun to his head or anything."

"I'll say," I agreed. I heaved a big sigh. "I suppose she started working on him while I was locked up in my bedroom. Modeling herself on me the way she did, it's no wonder he responded."

"Your parents *lock you up* in your bedroom?"

"Sure," I said, surprised that she was so shocked. "All the time. Don't yours?" In truth my parents hardly ever locked me up anymore, but I guess I'd assumed it was standard parenting practice when you caught your kid doing something wrong.

She shook her head. *"No! Never!"*

I was about to reassure her that an upside-down bucket made a perfectly adequate escape route, but decided that it was better to have her feeling sorry for me. Instead I slipped in a little flattery.

"That's probably because you never do anything wrong," I said.

She blushed and wriggled all over like a puppy. "Oh, I do *too*! You just don't know me well enough!"

"Name something terrible you've done," I said. "One thing."

By the time Brooke had reviewed the entirety of her sixteen blameless years and dredged up a misty memory of "stealing" a quarter she'd found under a couch cushion at age five, new images had appeared on Facebook, and Janelle's stupid animation had vanished from sight and, I hoped, from memory.

5

"I'M SORRY, DEAR, BUT YOU REALLY DO HAVE to talk to your parents sometime, and I know they have something very particular to say to you." Auntie X was holding the phone out to me, with a look that was half-sympathetic and half-stern. It was three days later, and with every day that passed I was more and more reluctant to be ejected from this cozy nest. That Mrs. Barnes—what a cook! Her desserts especially were beyond fabulous. I was going to grow into Janelle's clothes if I didn't watch out.

For three nights in a row I had refused to utter a word to either of my alleged relatives when they'd called. A look at Auntie X's and Uncle X's faces—I really *was* going to have to figure out the names in this family sometime—suggested that my refusal was not going to be accepted one more time.

"Okay," I said. I started blinking my eyes fast and quivering my lips. I raised a hand to brush away a tear, in case I found myself able to produce one. I shifted my gaze to the floor as I reached out to take the phone.

"Hi," I whispered, my voice husky.

"Well, for goodness' sake, Janelle, it's about time!" said a snappy female voice from three thousand miles away.

I said nothing.

"If you can stop sulking for long enough to listen, I've got some news for you."

I waited, breathing into the mouthpiece.

An exasperated sigh came from the telephone. "Something unexpected has come up with your father's work. There are problems on the site in Brazil, and they want somebody from the firm to go down and shepherd them through the process. Your father was going to send one of the younger engineers down, but we've decided—since you're so nicely settled there in Albany and things are so quiet here for me—that I should shut the shop for the next three months and go with him. In a way it's a shame you couldn't have come, but there wouldn't have been a proper school, not where they spoke English, anyway, and it's not worth learning Portuguese for three months."

After a brief pause, sharply: "Are you there, Janelle?"

I'd been silent because I'd been trying to smother any sounds of glee on my end. Could this possibly get any better? Mommy and Daddy were leaving for Brazil! For three months! I turned my smile upside down and said glumly, "Uh-huh. I'm here."

"Your voice sounds funny. You're still pretty annoyed with us, I gather."

"Mmm-hmm."

"You should be grateful to have such a nice place to stay," she said in disapproving tones. "Your aunt and uncle are *dear* people, and they have a *lovely* home. I hope you're behaving yourself and helping out."

"Mmm-hmm."

"I do *not* care for the tone of your voice, young lady! When I think of the mistake you very nearly made! That boy—"

There was a silence after that. Then: "Hi, honey. It's Dad. Your aunt Antonia says you and Brooke are getting along well."

Aunt Antonia! *Thank you, thank you, "Dad"!* Since repeated "Mmm-hmms" had roused "Mom" to such a fury, I switched back to my other standby.

"Uh-huh." Then, greatly daring, I added in a near-whisper, "She's nice."

My brokenhearted murmurings evidently smote him with remorse. "Gee, honey, I'm sorry you're so down, but honestly, it will pass. You'll make some nice friends there in Albany, and someday you'll look back on this and you'll laugh. You'll think about the great time you had staying with your aunt and uncle—"

My uncle who? *C'mon, give me his name!*

"—and your cousin Brooke."

I already knew *her* name.

"You know your mother and I are only doing this for—"

"For my own good." I could not help finishing for him. It *did* seem to be a common parental refrain.

"Yes, honey, for your own good. Now listen. I'm glad we got to talk to you today, because we won't be able to very often in the next few months. The site is in Mato Grosso, which is pretty far inland. We'll be in the Pantanal, which is kind of like the Everglades in Florida. It's a huge wetland, with lots of wildlife. We'll take lots and lots of photos."

He blathered on for a while about the site and the problems involved in shipping generators through the swamp or something like that. I said "Uh-huh" every so often.

"I wish you could have come with us. I know you'd have loved the birds."

Who, me? Birds? Nuh-uh! Not unless you're talking about a nice roasted chicken with gravy and a side of stuffing. I did *not* want to spend three months in a swamp, that was for sure.

"Tell you what, I'll arrange for you to have your horse-back riding lessons there in Albany this fall. That will take your mind off your troubles. And maybe Brooke would like to learn too."

"*What?*"

"Sure," he said, pleased with himself. "That's a great idea. I'll offer to pay for Brooke, too. You girls can bond over saddles and reins. Let me talk to Uncle Karl."

My brain had split in two. One half was celebrating the revelation of Uncle X's name; the other half was screaming, *No, no, no! No horseback riding lessons!* The momentary distraction caused by this split was fatal. I found myself handing the phone over to Uncle Karl.

Uncle Karl chatted with Dad for a while, arguing over who was going to pay for Brooke's riding lessons. Naturally, Brooke immediately said that there was nothing that would please her more than spending her Saturdays galloping around on the back of a beast that weighs three quarters of a ton and could crush her like a soda can beneath one hoof.

Uncle Karl got off the phone and handed it back to me.

"Well, this is good-bye for a while, cupcake," said Dad. "You be a good girl and make me proud, okay?"

"Okay. Good-bye, Dad," I said glumly, not even both-ering to disguise my voice. However, this didn't matter; Dad was so pleased at having negotiated an amicable conversation with his rebellious daughter that he didn't pick up on any subtle differences in pitch or tone. "Say bye to Mom for me," I added quickly, not wanting to be handed back to the Ice Queen again.

Everybody was wreathed with smiles when we disconnected—Aunt Antonia, Uncle Karl, Cousin Brooke, and probably "Mom and Dad" in Los Angeles too. Everybody was beaming but me.

"This is going to be *so* much fun," squealed Brooke, bouncing up and down on the couch. "I always *wanted* to learn to ride."

"Yes, and Morgan already knows how, so she can give you pointers."

Ha! The closest I'd ever been to a horse had been when I was speeding by its pasture at sixty-five miles an hour on one of our rare outings in the country in my parents' ancient automobile.

Okay, you are probably thinking, "But you said that the cold are fearless!" I wasn't *afraid* of riding a horse. It was more like I was *offended* by it. How dumb is it to revert to such an outmoded form of transportation? We have *cars*.

Also, I have noticed that animals, even stupid gushy dogs like golden retrievers and labs, don't take to me much. It's funny . . . people are supposed to be so much smarter than other animals, but I find it's a lot easier to fool a teacher than a spaniel.

So I was wondering what a big powerful horse might

do with a passenger that it didn't like. Probably find a way to lose the passenger. I needed to stay in control, and I was going to have to use different techniques to manipulate a horse from the ones I used on Brooke.

I asked Google how to solve this problem, and sure enough, there were plenty of instructional videos on YouTube. The most helpful, believe it or not, was a Disney cartoon called "How to Ride a Horse." Once you had gotten over the fact that the would-be horseback rider was this weird-looking dog named Goofy, there was actually a lot of useful information offered.

For instance, there was a discussion of the clothes you should wear—high boots, red jacket, hard hat, and riding crop. Personally, I'd have been happy to dispense with every single one except the last. I wanted that crop, which I immediately recognized as a tool for persuading the horse to do what I wanted, instead of what it wanted.

When I tentatively approached Aunt Antonia about a riding outfit, she and Brooke both immediately agreed that it would be much more fun to do it right, with the correct costume.

"And I *love* those boots," Brooke added as we perused the riding goods available for purchase online.

I had to admit that the knee-high boots in combination with the skintight chaps and tailored jacket were a good look. For some reason none of the jackets were the scarlet swallowtails that Goofy sported, but they were handsome anyway.

"And the hard hat sounds like a good safety precaution," added Aunt Antonia. "Like wearing a helmet on a bicycle."

I strongly suspected that Brooke, and possibly Aunt Antonia as well, would be softhearted when it came to animals, so I did not even mention the crop until we were almost done ordering. The crops were by far the cheapest part of the whole getup (those boots were nearly four hundred dollars a pair!), so it was easy to say, "Oh, and we'd better have a crop, too" right before we checked out.

I was right about Brooke.

"Oh, I don't want to *hit* the poor horse!" she objected.

I repeated the wisdom I had gleaned from another video—not Goofy this time. "You don't *hit* them. You *tap* them with it to let them know they can't do stuff like eating grass."

"But why shouldn't the horse eat grass if it's hungry?"

I rolled my eyes. Brooke was going to be a total pushover, I could see. With any luck she would be such a bad rider that the instructor's attention would be entirely on her, and my own performance would pass unnoticed.

6

I WAS RIGHT. I WAS A STAR AT HORSEBACK riding. Brooke was more like a burned-out asteroid.

The riding clothes arrived on Friday; our first lesson was on Saturday, and school would begin the following Wednesday. On Saturday morning bright and early we drove out to Hidden Hollow Ranch, the riding stables where we were to be introduced to the world of equestrians. It was the sort of day that makes people like Brooke get all lyrical and poetic.

"How perfectly lovely it is!" she rhapsodized as we sailed over little green hills in the Miata. "The sky is the color of a robin's egg, and the air tastes like wine!"

"How would *you* know?" I inquired, raising skeptical eyebrows.

"I have *too* drunk wine," she protested. "Lots of times. Mom and Dad give me a glass at Thanksgiving every year. And champagne for New Year's. I don't much like it, except for the champagne," she admitted.

"So, the air this morning tastes like the awful stuff your parents force you to drink on Thanksgiving?"

"Oh, Morgan! You know what I mean," she said, laughing at me. "It's in-*tox*-icating!" she sang out as she rounded a curve.

Once we got to the stable—a long, low, white building and accompanying farmhouse-type dwelling with assorted dogs and chickens prowling around—we were welcomed by the proprietor, one Ms. Bunce. *Ms. Bounce*, I thought as she showed us over the place and introduced us to our rides for the morning. Everything about her bounced: her walk, her voice, her ponytailed hair. Or maybe she looked as though she were riding a horse while actually striding around on her own two feet. She was about forty and in pretty decent shape for her age; apparently, riding horses is good for the figure. She looked like she wouldn't take much guff from anybody, either human or horse. I made a mental note to be careful with her.

Brooke was over the moon with delight at the softness of the horses' noses, the "intelligence" and "nobility" of their gaze, and the pleasure of feeding them carrots and some old mushy apples.

I kept my hands to myself and did not look directly at any of the animals until Bounce indicated which one was to be my mount. "Chessie" was her name—a shortening, Bounce explained, of the word "chestnut," as that was her coloration, with a white splash on the forehead.

Bounce brought the two horses outside and began to saddle up Brooke's, talking about the proper way to do it the whole time. I watched and listened carefully.

"So, I understand you've ridden before, Morgan," said Bounce.

"Some," I admitted, not wanting to appear too expert.

"Really? I got the impression you were pretty good."

"Oh, you know." I shrugged.

"Western or English?" she asked.

What? Western or English what?

However, I had to choose; she was waiting for an answer. Well, I myself was Western, being from California. Goofy the dog must be Western, since he was created by Walt Disney in Hollywood.

"Western," I decided.

"Okay. The only thing is, we mostly ride English around here. I have a Western saddle, but I gave it to your friend. I think it's easier for first-timers, to give them a taste of riding, and then, if they like it, we switch them over to English tack. How'd you like to learn English?"

Only a second's thought convinced me that this was

a gift. If I was learning a new style, no one could blame me for making mistakes.

"I would be happy to," I said graciously.

The English saddle was smaller, I could see. I also noticed that the Western saddle had a lovely thing sticking up in the front by which you could hold on. *My* saddle had no such convenient handle; I would have to manage without. In any case, both horses were soon ready to ride.

"Always approach the horse with a confident attitude," was the advice given in the Goofy cartoon. Well, that was easy enough. My entire attitude toward life is confident. I understand that when ordinary people are faced with something they fear, they feel sick to their stomach and begin to sweat. Not me. The closest thing to fear I have ever known is a nagging suspicion that I am about to get caught, which simply makes me irritable.

I therefore walked up to Chessie and took control of her bridle, fixing her with a long, unsmiling stare. She sidled away from me to the length permitted by the bridle and then cast nervous glances at Bounce, and at Brooke's horse, both of whom were preoccupied with Brooke. No help there. She looked back at me.

Way back when I'd met that carnie guy, he'd told me that he recognized me for what I was because I "had that stare." Now I knew what he meant. It's a predator's stare; the stare a wolf trains on the deer it plans to eat for dinner. I kept looking at Chessie for several seconds longer, conveying the message, *Screw with me, horse, and you'll live to regret it.*

She shivered all over and then lowered her head. She was still shooting little looks at me from time to time, but she stood meekly, waiting for me to mount.

Brooke naturally got lots of assistance mounting, while I was expected to take care of this myself, being an experienced rider. I decided to get it over with while everyone was distracted by Brooke's flailing around.

"Stay still," I ordered Chessie in a stern undertone. I took a good grip of the saddle, stuck my left foot up into the left-side stirrup, and launched myself upward. Chessie stood like a statue beneath me as I pivoted and came to rest on her back, facing forward and astride.

Easy peasy.

"Good horse," I said in a complacent tone. Chessie shivered again and turned her head to see what I was up to. I inserted my right foot into the right stirrup and gathered up the reins, letting go of the saddle. In order to feel secure and remain upright, I discovered, you had to grip with your legs.

A muffled shriek attracted my attention.

Brooke was in trouble. Bounce had had to call for assistance, and she held the horse still while two stable employees attempted to shove Brooke up onto the saddle. I watched her struggles with a pitying smile.

"Oh, please hold still, Miss Delilah," pleaded Brooke. ("Miss Delilah" being the ridiculous name of Brooke's steed.)

"She *is* holding still, at least so long as you don't knee her in the stomach, poor girl," said Bounce. "Let's try again. One, two, three and . . . up!"

This time the little group of assistants managed to get Brooke up onto Miss Delilah's back. "Perhaps a pony next time," mused Bounce. "Okay, now let go of the horn." As Brooke simply looked dazed, Bounce explained. "The horn! That thing on the pommel. The thing you're holding in a death grip. Let go!"

"*Let go?*" Brooke stared at Bounce disbelievingly.

"Yes. You need to hold on to the horse with your thighs, not your hands. You have to have your hands free for the reins."

"Oh. Okay," she said without enthusiasm.

After she had complied and taken up the reins, Bounce took a moment to turn around and check to see how I was doing. The stable help did as well.

I sat up a little straighter. I was conscious that I made rather a handsome picture—particularly in contrast to Brooke's sweaty terror—erect, calm, and composed in the saddle. Bounce nodded approvingly.

"Very nice. I can see you're an old hand. Brooke, watch your cousin. She knows what she's doing."

I smiled. And to think I owed it all to Goofy.

Once Bounce had slung herself across a big white animal, we began to move toward the riding ring. Miss Delilah interrupted our progress by halting and beginning to eat grass. Brooke watched her helplessly.

Bounce ordered, "Don't let her eat, Brooke! You have to show her you're in charge. Give her a dig with your heels. A little harder. Brooke, she's taking advantage of you."

Needless to say, Brooke had been relieved of her crop during the mounting fiasco, but I had retained mine. While we were standing around waiting for Brooke to deal with Miss Delilah's snack, my horse thought, for one split second, of taking a bite of grass herself. I transferred the reins into one hand and lowered the crop so it made contact with Chessie's flank. I bent forward over her neck and growled deep in my throat, but softly, so that only she and I could hear. Her head jerked back up, and she stood stone-still, the picture of equine good manners.

As it happened, Bounce had looked over at that moment. Too far away to hear the growl, she'd only seen my slight use of the crop, and that I had spoken to the horse. Clearly pleased, she nodded at me again.

The whole lesson went like that. It turned out that what Goofy was doing in that cartoon *was* English-style riding—I distinctly recalled the section where he was "rising to the trot," or "posting." After a few moments of feeling like a bowl of Jell-O falling down a flight of stairs, I found the rhythm, and was soon trotting fluidly around the ring. By listening carefully to Bounce's instructions to Brooke, I was able to unobtrusively adjust my grip on the reins and lower my heels so that I looked like a pro.

"Oh, excellent!" Bounce applauded my performance. She had had to lead Miss Delilah in a trot around the ring, with Brooke sliding first to one side, and then to the other, so I suppose our instructor was pleased not to have two incompetents on her hands.

Surprisingly, Brooke had conquered her panic and was beginning to have fun, despite slopping around on the horse's back like a sack of laundry. She looked awful, with her hair escaped from its barrette, her face bright red, and a roll of flesh showing beneath her jacket, but from time to time nervous giggles escaped her.

"I'm getting it, I'm getting it," she cried in triumph as she completed what I could tell was a bone-jarring circuit, whereupon she nearly fell off backward. Capitalizing on this diversion, Miss Delilah promptly stopped short and began to snatch at the tall grass that was poking through the fence.

"Sit up straight and grip with your thighs!" called Bounce. "Don't let her eat grass!" And so on.

Finally, evidently feeling that she had spent quite enough time on Brooke, our teacher told her to wait while she worked with me. She had a few corrections to offer, and a little advice. Mostly, though, she was content to watch me as I trotted gracefully past.

"You've got an excellent seat, and a real ability to move as one with the horse," she said. "I love to see it, you know. It's like one of those mind-melds when a really good rider is in the saddle. It's obvious when somebody's got a strong love of horses and the experience to back it up."

Chessie shook her head violently and whickered in disagreement. I could see the whites of her eyes, which I suspected signaled fear. She gazed longingly back at the stable but was too nervous of me to do anything more than look.

I smiled and thanked Bounce. Once again, humans were proving themselves inferior to the lesser animals when it came to figuring me out. Having made her mind up about me, Bounce was ignoring what her own horse was trying to tell her. Not that it mattered. My feelings toward Chessie were perfectly friendly, so long as she did what I told her to do.

"Perhaps you could show me your canter," Bounce was beginning, to my dismay, as I couldn't quite remember what a canter was, when she interrupted herself. "No, we haven't any time, sorry. I've got some more students arriving in about fifteen minutes, and we'll need to show Brooke how to see to her horse after a ride. Next week we'll have a look at your canter. I've no doubt we'll have you galloping and jumping in no time, if you haven't already mastered those skills."

Modestly I denied any knowledge of these evidently more advanced forms of riding.

"Uh-huh," said Bounce, smiling. "Like you've only ridden '*some*.'"

Chessie was reluctant to share the close confines of a stall with me while I brushed her, but I fixed her with another *Do as I say* stare, and she consented, heaving an obvious sigh of relief as I left and flipped the latch down on the door.

"Bye, Chessie," I said aloud. "See you next week."

She snorted. *Not if I see you first,* seemed to be her response.

In the next stall Brooke was still fussing over Miss Delilah. "What great big brown eyes you have, Miss Delilah dear," she crooned as she smoothed the horse's forelock. Honestly, it was like a little girl brushing her dolly's hair. She finally put down the currycomb and emerged from the stall.

We had both, it seemed, substantially changed our opinions about horseback riding.

"Do you know, I thought it would be much easier," Brooke confided. "I mean, I figured, how hard could it be? I assumed it would be like sitting on a moving sofa. But I think I'm getting it. *You*, of course, were wonderful! I know your dad said you were pretty good, but wow! You could tell that Ms. Bunce was impressed."

And *I* was far more favorably inclined to the exercise than I thought I'd be. Making a large, powerful creature like that obey me with nothing more than the force of my personality was a real kick. In-*tox*-icating, as Brooke would say.

"Good-bye, girls!" Bounce looked up and waved to us from where she was greeting the new students. "Morgan, be sure to explain to Brooke what she can expect to be feeling for the next few days, won't you?"

I said "Um-hmm" in return and waved.

"What did she mean?" demanded Brooke as she seated herself at the wheel of the Miata. "Wow, I sure am tired! Who'd have thought that riding a horse for an hour would be so exhausting! What is it that I can expect to be feeling for the next few days?"

Since I hadn't the foggiest idea, I contented myself with a mysterious smile.

"Wait and see," I said, and no matter how much Brooke begged for information, I stood my ground and refused to say another word on the subject.

7

THE NEXT MORNING I WOKE IN AGONY. MUSCLES
I had not even known existed throbbed and ached in
my back, my arms, and my stomach. But mostly, my
inner thighs were on fire. I groaned as I turned over in
bed.

A knock came on my bedroom door. "Yaghwah?" I
muttered in response, struggling to come to a seated
position.

A hunched and broken figure shuffled in through
the doorway. "Is this," the figure whispered, "what she
meant?"

"What *who* meant?" I demanded, having managed
to sit up in my bed.

"Ms. Bunce. She told you to warn me about what

to expect I'd be feeling in the next few days."

Oh, right. The hunched, pathetic figure was Brooke. And we were both apparently experiencing the same misery of sore muscles after our first hour astride a horse. Only she was not supposed to realize that it was *my* first hour.

"What, are you *sore*?" I asked, trying to sound carefree and at ease.

"Oooh," she groaned, collapsing onto my bed. "Ow, ow, ow! Yes, I am sore," she said mournfully.

I pasted a superior smile on my face. "I suppose you would be. All first-timers get it. You see," I said, making it up as I went along, "you're exercising muscles while riding a horse that you normally don't use. So after your first time it hurts."

Actually, my explanation made sense.

"But . . . but it gets better, right?" Brooke said in a pleading tone. "I mean, as you ride regularly, you get used to it and your muscles get stronger, right? *You* feel okay, don't you?"

"Well," I said, "I haven't ridden in a few weeks because of being locked up in my room, so, yeah, I'm a *little* sore. Not as bad as you are, of course, but I can feel it too."

"What do we do?" she asked plaintively. "How do I get back to feeling human again?"

"First, two ibuprofen and a hot shower, and then, later, the sauna," I said. I could tell this was the right idea—just the thought of hot steam made me feel better.

She thought so too. "Oooh, a hot shower! Yes! And then the sauna! Oh, you are so right, Morgan. Okay, see you."

In my old house in Los Angeles we had only one bathroom, so Brooke and I would have had to wait and take turns after the parents were done, and I won't bore you with the blah-blah-blah yelling about my long, hot showers. In this house every bedroom had a bath, and there was no drought to impose restrictions, so we both climbed into our showers at about the same time. And of course, my old house didn't have a sauna.

There were mounds of blueberry pancakes on the table when we came down for breakfast, with sausages and sliced fruit. We fell upon the feast like hungry wolves.

"Hey, easy, tigers," said Uncle Karl. It was a Sunday, so he was allowing his underlings to write up the contracts at his various dealerships and was instead lounging around at home in a bathrobe so luxurious that it looked like it had been fashioned from the rarest of endangered animal hair. "Don't eat the plates. What are you two up to today?"

"I don't know about Morgan, but I'm going to stay home and recuperate. She's fine—she's hardly sore at all."

"Oh, I was hoping to go clothes shopping with you girls," cut in Aunt Antonia. "Are you sure you're not up to it, Brooke?"

Brooke's only response was a groan.

"Well, it's really only Morgan who needs new clothes, so I suppose she and I can go alone just as well. Not as much fun for her, maybe, but school starts next Wednesday, so she needs something that fits."

I closed my eyes briefly to gather strength. Under any other circumstances I would have adored being taken out shopping for clothes, with or without Brooke. In fact, without Brooke there to possibly sop up some of her mother's generosity, I would probably wind up getting more stuff. Today, though, I sure wouldn't have minded spending the afternoon cycling in and out of the sauna, instead of tramping all over the mall and undressing and redressing countless times in tiny changing booths.

"I'd love to," I said with a brave smile. "Thank you so much, Aunt Antonia."

"Actually, I'm not entirely sorry we're going to have this time alone together, Morgan," Aunt Antonia said.

Uh-oh. I smiled vaguely at her as she swung the Cadillac into the mall parking lot. *That* sounded like trouble.

She sat motionless, not moving to open her door. I considered making a bolt for it and pretending I didn't know that she wanted to talk, but decided that it would just be postponing whatever it was, and that she would be more likely to be openhanded in buying me goodies if not distracted by other concerns.

"I hope that you are settling in with us, Morgan," she began.

That was easy.

"Oh yes! I love it here," I said with enthusiasm.

"I was concerned by our conversation a few days ago. I don't know your parents well—living on opposite sides of the country, we don't see too much of them—but I do know that Karl says they love you very much." She stopped, evidently trying to figure out what to say next.

I thought this over. Let's see . . . I tried to remember what Brooke had said. If Aunt Antonia didn't know *either* of Janelle's parents well, she couldn't be a sister to one of them. So . . . that meant that easygoing Uncle Karl was the brother of the Ice Queen? Weird, if true, but I thought that was right.

My conversation with Brooke on the way home from the airport flashed back over me. Hadn't I hinted that my father had an ungovernable temper? Remembering the guy I talked to the other day on the phone, this seemed unlikely to actually be true. Maybe I'd better be careful. It was the Ice Queen who seemed most prone to losing it, and probably her brother, Uncle Karl, knew it.

I decided to go for an emerging-maturity kind of tone. I let out a long sigh.

"Oh, I suppose they do. It's just . . . you know, they have weird ways of showing it. And I don't think that they consider what effect their forms of discipline are going to have on me."

"Forms of discipline . . . ," Aunt Antonia said. "Yes, that was what worried me. I didn't mention the need for this shopping trip to your parents. I didn't know how to broach the subject of how much weight you appear to have lost lately."

I nodded my approval. "Yeah, probably better not to. They're kind of sensitive about it."

Aunt Antonia pounced, as if this was a valuable admission on my part. "But why? Why should they be sensitive about it?"

I dropped my gaze and looked evasive.

"Because. I don't know. They don't want people thinking they put undue pressure on me, I guess." I turned my head to stare out the side window, body language signaling an unwillingness to discuss this subject any further.

Aunt Antonia was silent. Then she said slowly, "All right. I suppose we'll leave it at that. But you know, Morgan, if ever you want to talk, I am happy to listen. As you might expect, I have quite a bit of experience with this sort of thing, given my job."

Eh? Somehow I'd gotten the idea she worked in an office somewhere shuffling papers. Or . . . I don't know, as the browbeaten secretary in a pencil factory. Could she be a guidance counselor?

She put her hand on the car door handle, and I relaxed, thinking the interrogation was over.

"Your parents didn't know about the name change," she said, without opening the door. "Neither had ever heard you express any dissatisfaction with your name or interest in changing it. They wondered where you had gotten the idea."

"They don't know everything there is to know about me," I said, which was entirely accurate.

She sighed. "I suppose that's true. Well, let's get shopping." Finally, *finally* she got out of the car, and I followed suit. Still, she looked at me over the roof as we shut the doors, a long, long look that I did not entirely know how to interpret.

Oh well. Whatever.

I knew it was going to be *so* much easier for me to turn over a new leaf and stop stealing things here; I had everything I could possibly want! Designer clothes, new haircut (Aunt Antonia insisted, and I looked *great!*), new shoes (Aunt didn't seem to think much of the ones I was wearing), even a pretty little gold necklace. True, I didn't have a phone, but what of it? I'm not social, I don't play games, and I don't listen to music, so it wasn't as big a deal to me as it would be to most teenage girls. And if I behaved myself and didn't hook up with any inappropriate boys, I bet Auntie would eventually be persuaded to come across with one. Assuming I decided I wanted one.

The only thing I regretted about our shopping spree was that I didn't feel well enough to milk Aunt Antonia for all she was worth. As I'd anticipated, taking clothes off and putting them on multiple times was painful, and I wasn't able to enjoy the experience as much as I would have liked. Buying jeans was the worst. Toward the end she thought I should try on another pair, and I could not do it. The only thing I wanted was to get back home to the bottle of ibuprofen in my bathroom.

"No thanks," I said, and since there was no way I could benefit any further from her largess at the moment, I added cunningly, "You have been more than generous. I couldn't possibly accept anything else."

"Oh, think nothing of it, dear," said Aunt Antonia. "It's a pleasure buying clothes for a girl who enjoys them. Brooke isn't interested." She unlocked the trunk of the Cadillac so I could store my bags of wonderful new things. "You've got a great figure for clothes, and good taste, too. I used to be fond of new things myself, but in my line of work you have to be conservative, and nobody ever notices what you're wearing anyway."

One of these days I was going to have to figure out what Aunt did for a living. *Could she possibly be a lady minister?* I laughed aloud.

She smiled back at me and said, "We're so happy to

have you here, Morgan. Brooke was terribly nervous about you coming, you know, but she's very pleased about it now. I think this is going to work out well for both of you girls."

Really? Brooke was terribly nervous about my coming? I wondered why. Secrets to hide, perhaps?

"She'll be able to take you around to your classes when school starts and introduce you to everyone. I know it's always hard to start at a new school. You're registered, by the way. It was a bit of a rush, since everything was decided only a few days ago. But your mother managed to get a package of your documents to me Express Mail, so we're all set."

Documents?

"I never thought of that," I said.

"Oh yes, they're strict here. Your parents had to grant us legal custody to ensure that you were able to go to school in our district. My being a psychiatric social worker for the state helped too, I think."

A *what*? Boring old Auntie was a psychiatric social worker? Hmm. Maybe I shouldn't underestimate her powers of penetration. Surely she had run into others of my kind before.

"And naturally the school wanted a copy of your transcript and immunization record," she concluded.

So Uncle and Aunt-the-psychiatric-social-worker were my legal guardians, were they? Interesting. I would have to store that little tidbit in the back of my mind and think about it later.

I couldn't see how any of Janelle's documents would get me in trouble. I don't think you can tell by looking at someone whether or not they've been vaccinated for measles. And as for Janelle's grades, well, she didn't seem awfully bright to me, so unless she'd been hiding a massive intellect under that flaky personality, that wouldn't be a problem—

"And of course," continued Aunt Antonia, casting a swift glance at me as she pulled out into traffic, "we are hoping that, since you will have no *distractions* here, you'll be able to bring your grade point average up a bit."

Aaah. I smiled beatifically. Good old Ashton-the-distraction. It looked like I was going to be able to better Janelle's performance in the classroom with the greatest of ease.

8

JUST LIKE IN BROOKE'S NEIGHBORHOOD, THE high school grounds were one gigantic lawn, and there was hardly any chain-link fencing there, either. Yeah, the tennis court was fenced in, but the whole, sprawling campus was not, unlike my school in LA. Brooke's school was wide open, so that anybody could walk in. People around here seemed to be awfully trusting, like nobody would ever need to be excluded, nobody would ever think to do anything bad. I suppose that's the difference between the city and the suburbs; people in the suburbs think they have put enough distance between themselves and evil so that they can relax. In my opinion, though, greed and selfishness are a basic part of human nature. People can move away as far as they like, but their vices will come slinking along after them like a pack of half-tamed pariah dogs.

My old school wasn't bad. It sent a lot of kids on to college and met most of the state competency requirements even though an awful lot of the student body qualified for free lunches. You could tell that the average family income in this district was a lot higher. The cars in the parking lots were nicer, and so were the clothes worn by both faculty and students. I wasn't used to so many people being white-bread-white either, even though I am pretty white-bread-white myself. There was a scattering of black and brown faces in the halls here, but most of the students looked like they'd blister and burn after twenty minutes in direct sunlight. Coming here from Southern California, this place had the look of a school in a 1950s teen movie.

But who cares about the differences? School is school is school. So long as the class work wasn't a whole lot harder, I'd survive all right. I always do.

It was a lucky thing that Janelle was such a dope and expectations of me were therefore low. It *was* harder here. Well, for one thing, I skipped a full academic year because Janelle is six months older than I am. And I supposedly had two years of French under my belt. Forget that. I said I hated French and wanted to switch to

Spanish. Janelle was failing anyway, so that made sense.

But the math and literature classes were way harder than I'd expected, and instead of being goof-off periods like they were in my old school, you were actually expected to work in art and gym. Spanish was easy. I'd been taking it anyway, and living in LA, you absorb some through your pores.

The thing was, I had a moment when I totally blanked out on "my" last name. Janelle— Um . . . yeah. I knew it—it was on her driver's permit—but I hadn't used it since I'd been here, so I sat there staring at the form I was filling out. Good thing Aunt Antonia had filled out nearly everything already. I had no idea what school I'd supposedly gone to, or where I'd been born or any of that stuff.

Finally it came to me: Janelle Johanssen. Right. With a double *s* and an *e* not an *o*. I wrote it out as: "Morgan (Janelle) Johanssen." I wasn't going to be called Janelle by all these people.

So far as social interactions went that first day, I sat back and watched as Brooke did her thing. It was hard to guess what place Brooke would occupy in the hierarchy. She was not bad-looking, even if kind of chubby, her family was rich, and she was in advanced placement classes. But she was clueless when it came to any kind of street smarts; she assumed everyone was like her, well-intentioned, friendly, and bubbly. She did not even seem to know that there *was* a hierarchy. I could tell that some of her dear friends, if they thought it would do them any good with the most popular crowd, would drop her so fast, she'd bounce. She obviously had no idea.

Personally, I didn't care about being in with the in crowd. I like being by myself, and have no need of peer approval to make me feel important. True, I wanted to be admired and respected here, but I didn't need to worry about hanging out with a bunch of other people just to avoid being alone.

Brooke, of course, thought that I must have felt terribly lonely and unsure of myself in a school where I knew no one, because that's the way she would feel in my place. Aunt Antonia had arranged for me to be in several of Brooke's classes and for us to share the same lunch period so I wouldn't be on my own too much. Brooke dragged me from one clump of people to another, introducing me as, "My cousin from LA. She's teaching me horseback riding, and she's *really* good!" Some of these people were obviously the elite, some were elite-wannabes, some run-of-the-mill, and some were hopeless losers. Brooke treated them all the same and acted like she thought they would all be equally thrilled to meet her horsey cousin from LA.

I nodded coolly, said hello and not much else. One girl who was apparently also into horses perked up at the mention of what a fabulous rider I was and started gabbling about dressage and point-to-points, whatever they were.

All in all, I was satisfied with my first day at school. I would have to watch the scene here for a week or two before I figured out where I would fit in best. Socializing does not come naturally to me; I have to study people to figure out what is motivating them and what they are thinking beneath the surface.

We already had a ton of homework—different again from my old school, where they let you off easy the first week—so we went straight home after school. After a snack of low-calorie dip and vegetables (Brooke was trying to lose a little weight, so I was condemned to diet food as well), we retired to our respective rooms and dug into the algebra problems our mutual math teacher had assigned.

At dinner that night the conversation was lively, with Aunt and Uncle asking a lot of questions and Brooke burbling away the way she usually did, about her friends, her new teachers, and her classes. Finally Aunt turned to me.

"And, Morgan, how about you? How did you like your first day?"

"Oh, Morgan is really smart, you can tell," put in Brooke before I could open my mouth. "She's in my economics class, and she gave a brilliant answer when Mr.

Humber asked us to discuss this quotation about how, when ethics and economics are in conflict, economics always win. She was ruthless! Wow, don't ever cross Morgan! I think you should be a lawyer, Morgan. You've got that kind of logical mind. Only, it seems to me like economics *have* to be guided by ethics, or we'll be living in a dog-eat-dog world where only the strong survive."

"We *are* living in a dog-eat-dog world where only the strong survive," observed Uncle Karl, the car-dealership king.

"Oh, Dad, we are not! You know you are much nicer than you give yourself credit for. You are a generous—"

"*Actually*, Brooke, Karl, I was asking *Morgan* how her day went," pointed out Aunt Antonia. I replied in a composed manner that it had gone well, and Uncle Karl and Brooke picked up their argument and battled it out amicably for another ten minutes.

"Any acts of generosity that I perform, I perform because they are in my own best interests," Uncle Karl was saying. "I treat my customers well so that they'll come back and buy another car from me in a few years. I treat my employees and suppliers well in order to make *my* life easier and my business more successful. Donations to charity are good for public relations because if people think you're a nice guy, they're more likely to stop by your dealership when they're in the market. It's enlightened self-interest."

This seemed entirely reasonable to me. In fact, I could not imagine what Brooke could see wrong in this; it's how the world works. Brooke thought that her father had a generous nature because he was generous to *her,* when, really, he was generous to her because she belonged to him. She had his genes; she was an aspect of him that would live on into the future after he was dead. He was really being good to *himself* when he saved up for her college education. He was ensuring that a part of him would survive and thrive.

Even Aunt Antonia's buying spree for me had been based on the same thing. Okay, she and Janelle didn't share any genes, but her husband and Janelle did, so it seemed right to her to spend his money on his sister's child, especially since there was lots to go around. If she'd had any idea who I really was, do you think she'd have showered me with all those lovely clothes? Not a chance. She'd have called the cops, more likely. I was like a parasitic cowbird's egg that had been laid in a finch's nest. If the finch mother had recognized me for what I was, she would have pushed me out and let me go *smash!* on the stones below.

Parents care about their kids because it's their chance at immortality. At least, that's the only way I can make sense of parents sacrificing for their children. If *I* had a kid, I don't know how generous *I'd* be. Don't worry; I'm not planning on becoming a mother, in either the near

DON'T YOU TRUST ME?

or distant future. But I guess it's reasonable that parents want their kids to do well in the world, if you look at it that way.

"*Mom*," Brooke was protesting. "You know that Dad is better than that! Stick up for me!"

"Your father is both a successful businessman and a decent human being, Brooke. He talks that way because he worries that you are too openhearted. He's afraid it makes you vulnerable to all the wickedness of the world."

"Mom! Dad! I'm not some little toddler anymore!" Brooke caught my eye, sitting quietly at my place at the table, and blushed, probably realizing that she sounded exactly like some little toddler. "And I don't believe that there *is* that much honest-to-goodness wickedness in the world," she said defiantly. "I think that if you could see into the inmost heart of a person who has done something really, really wrong, you would find that they were just—just misguided. It was because they had an awful childhood or something."

Well, if Brooke could see into my inmost heart, I supposed she would think I was doing something wrong by being here at her dinner table. And I couldn't claim to have had an awful childhood, so I had to beg to differ.

Uncle Karl was girding up his loins to march into battle again, when Aunt Antonia apparently decided that she had had enough of the subject. In any case, she headed him off by asking, "Morgan, where did you get that pretty gold chain? I don't remember seeing that before."

I glanced down at the chain around my neck. "Oh, I've had it for years," I said vaguely. "Could you pass the butter, please?"

Brooke looked surprised, either because I had just helped myself to some butter or perhaps because on the day after I arrived, she had, in her innocently curious way, looked over every single item Janelle had packed in her luggage. There had been no gold chain then. However, she evidently concluded that neither mystery was worth solving. I mean, a gold chain is a small thing, which might easily escape notice. She was soon diverted by a discussion about debate team, which her mother was anxious she join.

However, I can sense that *you*, my reader, may not be satisfied by my explanation. *You* remember what I said about that gold chain. I implied that Aunt Antonia had bought it for me. I also implied that because she was so generous, I had stopped taking things that didn't belong to me.

Well, it certainly wasn't *my* fault. We had gone into the jewelry store because Aunt Antonia'd had a repaired piece to pick up—a gruesome old-timey brooch. There were two clerks. One had brought a small rack of gold chains out to the counter to show to a customer. The customer tried a necklace on and moved to the mirror to admire it, and the clerk followed her. The other clerk went back behind the scenes to get Aunt's brooch, and Aunt's eyes were on her, not on me. One discarded necklace was lying on the counter, sitting in a ray of that high-intensity light that jewelry stores use, with nobody paying any attention either to it or to me. It *glittered* at me.

I mean, I don't know how anybody could have expected me *not* to snag it.

There was a camera mounted on the ceiling, of course—there always is—so I put my purse and one of my shopping bags on the counter, blocking the stray necklace from the camera's line of sight. Then I moved slowly down the line of glass cases, looking at the goodies inside. When Aunt Antonia finished up her business and looked at me, I "came to" out of my distraction. I hurried back to her, scooping up my belongings, and incidentally the necklace, as I followed her out of the store.

So I lied. Big deal.

9

"HOW ARE YOU GOING TO GET YOUR HOURS?"
Emma asked me, forking a green bean into her mouth.

It was lunchtime on Friday, the first week of school, and Emma, the horsey girl, had settled down to eat with Brooke and me. I raised inquisitive eyebrows.

"Hours?" I said.

"Lebanon Hill High School makes you do twenty hours of community service before you can graduate," she explained. "I'm going to work for the food pantry this afternoon. You two want to come?"

"Oh, I'd love to," Brooke said. "I volunteered at the homeless shelter last summer, but my father made me quit." She made a face. "He said he didn't care for the quality of people you meet at a homeless shelter."

Emma snorted into her milk carton. "No, I s'pose he wouldn't."

"*Volunteer?*" I said. As in, work without pay? Then it came back to me. They were doing the same thing in LA. You had to "volunteer" or you couldn't graduate. I nearly opened my mouth to assure them that I didn't have to worry about it yet, as I was only a sophomore, but I remembered in time that Janelle, and therefore *I*, was a junior.

"That sounds like a lot of fun," I said hastily, trying to cover up for my indignant query. Whoop-de-doo. A food pantry. Cans of brown and orange food. Reminders of how close my family had occasionally come to needing a bag full of free food at the end of the month.

"Actually, it is, kind of," said Emma. "Lots of hauling stuff around, but everybody's in a good mood, and the time goes fast. Sometimes we sing, you know, in rounds, like 'Row, Row, Row Your Boat,' if there are little kids there volunteering, or a cappella, if there are people who can sing."

"Oh, I can't hold a tune, but I'm sure it's great," said Brooke. "My dad wants me to volunteer at something cultural, like the museum or symphony. That's nice too, but I don't feel like I'm really helping people who need it."

"The pantry needs it, for sure. Donations are down, and we have to stock it up again. That's what we're doing today, actually, not working in the pantry itself but going around looking for donations. People almost always have extra stuff they don't need on their shelves. Sometimes it's, like, chocolate-covered ants or something, and we don't take it, but there's a ton of unopened food sitting around unused."

Not in *my* family's cupboards. There was never anything left over at our house. Now that I thought about the dreary round of scrimping and make-do that was so commonplace in my former home, it was odd that my parents could have afforded to send me away to school. I suppose they must have taken out a second mortgage on the house. Considered in that light, I had done them a big favor by disappearing the way I had. With me gone, they wouldn't have to pay. My folks had kind of slipped my mind lately—there had been too much else going on—but I found myself feeling a little pleased to think they were better off now too. See? I'm not that bad a person. I can have generous thoughts.

Brooke's Miata was not ideal for the job at hand, which required seating three people and hauling a lot of canned goods, so Emma followed us home after school in her mom's Subaru wagon. Once we'd dropped off the car and our school stuff, we drove to Emma's neighborhood. There had been flyers distributed a few days before, announcing the food drive, and a few houses here and there had plastic bags hanging from doorknobs, or mailboxes with jars and boxes inside. We drove slowly around picking these up and packing them into the car.

Pretty soon we ran out of houses with bags outside. Emma heaved a big sigh and started complaining. "People are so *cheap*! Everybody in this neighborhood is making, like, a bazillion dollars a year, and they can't be bothered to put out a few cans of food *that they don't even want*, for charity. For people who don't have enough to eat!"

Naturally, Brooke was quick to defend Emma's neighbors.

"Emma, they probably forgot, that's all. We'll go back to my neighborhood and distribute flyers there. I'll bet we'll get *lots* of stuff."

To my amazement, I realized that Emma was actually in tears over this situation. I admit I didn't get it, but I was growing bored with the drama and the whole scene, so I decided to get some actual results.

"Wait here," I said, and climbed out of the car. I walked up to the last house we'd gotten a bag from and rang the doorbell. This time of day, four p.m., was a bit of a toss-up. Everybody might still be at work, or, on the other hand, not. However, I could see a car in the garage, so I figured it was worth a try.

Eventually my patience was rewarded.

"Yes?" The door opened wide enough so that I could see a late-forties-ish woman peering out at me.

I produced a winning, confident smile.

"Hi! I stopped to pick up your donation for the food pantry. We appreciate your generosity."

The woman's gaze dropped to the doorknob where the bag had been five minutes ago.

"But—but didn't you see the bag there on the knob?"

I made my face look confused: wrinkled brow, worried eyes.

"Well . . . yeah, I thought I did when we drove to the other end of the street. That's why I stopped. See, we parked down there, and we've been working our way back this way, picking up donations. I thought maybe you brought the bag back in to add some more stuff to it?" I smiled hopefully.

"No . . . no, I didn't. There wasn't much, just some soup my husband hates and some kind of Alfredo sauce that I never used. But I thought I saw somebody picking it up a minute ago. Somebody was on the porch, anyway."

This time my face crumpled with dismay. My whole body sagged. My mouth dropped open, and I willed moisture into my eyes.

"You mean—you mean somebody *stole* it?"

The door opened a little wider.

"I'm sure nobody would steal a bag with two cans of soup and a jar of Alfredo sauce. It was probably another of your helpers, and you didn't notice."

I shook my head. I pointed at Emma's car, two houses

down the road. Emma and Brooke obligingly stuck their heads out the windows and looked at me with puzzled expressions, not sure what I was up to. Their faces were little more than pink ovals from here, so the woman wasn't about to recognize either of them.

"None of us took it. Oh, that is so awful! People can be so awful!" I wailed. I allowed my voice to crack a little on the last "awful." "You can't trust *anybody*!"

"Well, what a shame. You poor thing! Here, why don't you come in for a moment?" She stepped out onto the porch and waved reassuringly at Emma and Brooke. I also turned and smiled at them before being ushered into the house.

"Look, I'm sure I can rustle up some more things for you. Really, I'm a bit ashamed I gave so little. When I think about you girls out on your own time doing volunteer work like this—you *are* volunteers, aren't you?"

"Yes, ma'am. We're students at the high school. We want to do our part for the community. There are people our age who won't have anything to eat for dinner tonight. I think about that when I'd rather hang out with my friends or go clothes shopping, you know?"

The woman, who was dressed like she did plenty of shopping herself, looked stricken. "Honestly, you're making me feel absolutely terrible. Here, I think I have a cardboard box we can use. Come into the pantry. Let's see what we can spare. Look, there're lots of things, now

I consider it. Hmm . . . these cans of salmon and tuna would be good, wouldn't they? And here are some wonderful soups. I love the lobster bisque and the mock turtle, myself. Oh, and do you think anyone would like some smoked oysters? It's kind of an acquired taste, I suppose, but it *is* protein, isn't it?"

Once we had decimated her stock of canned goods, we moved on to cereals, pancake mixes, macadamia nuts, and evaporated milk. Soon I was staggering under the weight of the groceries, and my new friend guided me back to the front door.

"Oh! Can you wait a second? I'd like to give you a check, too. Let's see, I should make it out to—"

It was actually probably a good thing that at that moment she spotted the handout Emma had left a few days ago and used it to copy down the proper name on the check. Otherwise I might have been tempted to divert the funds to myself. I mean, I did get all that food for the poor starving children. I deserved *something* for my trouble, right?

She tucked the check in under one of the cans and waved me off cheerfully as I stammered my thanks.

"No, thank *you*! It cheers me up to see such outstanding kids in my neighborhood. Bye! Bye-bye, girls!"

Brooke and Emma got out of the car to help stow the carton in the trunk. Wide-eyed, they goggled at the check, which was for two hundred dollars.

"What did you say to her?"

Mentally I reviewed the conversation. It is my principle to try to tell the truth where possible.

"I thanked her for her donation," I said. "I told her how much we appreciated it. She asked if we were volunteers. Then she thought she might have some other stuff in the kitchen, so we went in and looked around in her pantry. Do you think the homeless will eat smoked oysters?"

Brooke was elated at my cleverness. "Oh, Morgan, how wonderful! It's true, you should be a lawyer. You could talk a jury into anything!"

Emma was slightly more restrained. "So . . . you mean, what you did was, you walked up to her door like Oliver Twist with his empty bowl of gruel and said, 'May I have some more, please?'"

I considered this. "Yeah, basically," I agreed.

"Wow."

I smiled. "I could do it again, I bet." I said as they turned to me with hopeful faces, "No, not right here. How about driving a few blocks over to where we picked up some bags a while ago?" When they looked perplexed at this, I explained, "It needs to be the right kind of house and we need to see a car in the driveway or the garage so we know somebody's home."

They nodded, satisfied. Actually, I just didn't want Ms. Generous to look out her window and see us hitting up her neighbors the same way I'd hit her up.

In the end we got three more big boxes of food, two more checks, and two twenties (which I pocketed). I didn't use the "somebody stole your donation" line every time, for fear they'd know one another and compare notes. No, sometimes I pretended that I couldn't believe that absolutely nobody on their road had had the common decency to give unwanted canned items to charity and threatened to blubber all over them, while expressing my heartfelt belief that they were the only decent people in the whole neighborhood. None of the results were quite as spectacular as the first house, but they were solid donations.

Not a bad afternoon's work, and I was the unquestioned heroine of the hour.

Saturday morning, and we were up at dawn again, wending our way out to the stables. I had taken care to research cantering and galloping online beforehand. I thought I could manage them, being sure to blame any awkwardness on the fact that I was riding English style for the first time. The weather wasn't quite so idyllic this trip; there were ragged clouds racing across the sky, and the air felt damp with promised rain. Coming from the dry state of California, the dampness in the air felt good; I could feel my skin plumping up with moisture. Summer was gradually giving way to autumn, and the tips of the leaves were turning color.

Still, it stayed dry for our lesson. Amazingly, Brooke only required one stable hand to get her up on her horse. Bounce had offered her a pony, but she turned down the suggestion, sure she would succeed this time. Once again she wobbled around in the saddle (Bounce wasn't going to push her into an English saddle for a while yet) but managed a soggy trot several times around the ring as we watched and applauded. I tried my canter while Bounce was working with Brooke, and found it actually easier and smoother than the trot. It was faster, which I liked too.

Chessie had not been overjoyed to see me but had apparently decided that I was relatively harmless so long as she appeased me with strict obedience, which was precisely what I wanted. She seemed familiar with the canter, and as soon as I clucked at her and dug my heels in, she broke into a nice rocking rhythm that carried us rapidly around the ring.

"Great job!" bellowed Bounce from her position aiding Brooke.

The next day when I woke up, I was hardly sore at all.

And that was pretty much how that whole week had gone. I wasn't only managing to avoid detection and expulsion; I was making an enormous success of my new life.

10

MY FAME AS A FUND-RAISER SPREAD LIKE A forest fire up a parched hillside. When I returned to school on Monday, it had preceded me.

"Excuse me, but are you Morgan Johanssen?" A dark girl with glasses and an intense expression stepped out in front of me as I walked toward my locker before homeroom.

I was about to reply in the affirmative when another girl, this one with lots of red hair and makeup, dressed in a weird outfit that looked like it had been formed out of black duct tape, cut in.

"Serena Jones, don't you *dare*! You know perfectly well it was my idea to talk to her about raising money for the art festival!"

"The animal shelter needs the money a lot more!"

Now Emma was approaching, with a look of thunder on her face.

"No poaching, Serena, Melanie. Morgan is collecting money for the *food pantry*!"

"I hear she already did! Why can't you share the wealth, Emma?" demanded the duct tape girl, who must have been Melanie.

"Well, hello, ladies," drawled a voice coming from somewhere near the ceiling. I looked up. Sandy hair, blue eyes, a lazy grin, all attached to a male body that just wouldn't quit. He must have been at least six foot five, I decided, and every inch of him was a tribute to good nutrition and keeping fit. Craning my neck, I smiled up at him. I was the only one doing this, however. The other three "ladies" were looking annoyed.

"The basketball team sure doesn't need a fund-raiser," Melanie blurted out. "The taxpayers give you guys a free ride, practically."

Blue Eyes lifted his eyebrows. "A fund-raiser? Sorry, not sure what you're talking about. I stopped by to say hello to the new member of our academic community. Morgan, isn't it? The name is Brett Elway."

"Hello, Brett," I said, looking at him from under my lashes. My, but he was tall!

"I suppose you're after money for away-game transportation and uniforms," Melanie said bitterly. "In art club we have to pay for every little thing. Why can't your parents chip in? Or why can't you get a job after school to pay for that stuff?"

Brett turned and regarded her with a wondering gaze. "And miss practice? What would be the point in that?"

"Notice he's not denying it anymore, Morgan," said Emma. "They're all of them after you for one thing, so don't think it's because they *like* you!"

I said nothing but gazed at her, wide-eyed. She blushed.

Brooke had been hovering near us, listening. Now she burst in with, "I'm sorry, Emma, but I think you all are being . . . being—" Brooke halted, thwarted by her inability to say anything even slightly critical to anyone. She tried again, and put her back into it this time.

"Here Morgan is, brand-new to our school, making a huge effort to help out and do good in a community where she just moved. And what do we do? We act like she's a commodity that one of us can gain a monopoly over. *Poor Morgan!* How do you think this is making her feel?"

Poor Morgan was feeling like she had never in her life been so popular and so in demand.

However, the girls in our group were looking a bit abashed at this extremely mild tongue-lashing. Only Brett seemed unfazed by Brooke's scolding. He went on smiling his sunny smile and regarding me with big blue eyes. Undoubtedly this tactic had worked his whole life and he saw no reason to alter it now.

"Maybe," I said, smiling around at my circle of admirers, "I can help you all."

This charity scheme was wonderful. Not only was it going to help me achieve my goal of being admired and respected, but I got to rake off any cash donations into my own pocket. Sure, *some* people might have gotten greedy and wanted a larger cut of the take, but I figured that since my basic needs were being catered to so well by Brooke's family, I didn't *need* a lot of money. Janelle's parents had apparently given Aunt and Uncle some funds for a weekly allowance for me. It was three times the amount my own parents used to dole out. What with that and a twenty here and a twenty there from my charity work, I would be doing quite well.

On the other hand there was my future to think about. It wouldn't do to be *too* generous.

"The important thing," I explained to my friends-in-philanthropy at lunchtime, "is that we don't want a particular neighborhood suffering from donor-fatigue, so we can't squeeze anybody too hard. The image we are projecting is of a bunch of kindhearted, well-intentioned teenagers collecting for a good cause."

Emma narrowed her eyes. "We *are* a bunch of kindhearted, well-intentioned teenagers collecting for a good cause," she pointed out. "Or at least Serena and Brooke and I are. Brett and Melanie want somebody to underwrite their after-school activities."

I waited for Melanie's furious riposte on the deplorable state of the arts in America to die down before responding.

"Of course we are," I agreed. "And we don't want anybody to get any other ideas. What I want to do is a kind of charitable carpet bombing. We six descend on a neighborhood, fan out, and hit every house. If you see people in their gardens or yards or garages, go and talk to them. It should be on Saturday, not a weekday afternoon, so people are home. We can make it after our horseback riding lesson, Brooke. We should try a different neighborhood this week and not go back to yours, Emma, until we've extracted everything we can get from the other developments. And don't forget—guilt is an important motivator, and donations from upper-income families are likely to be bigger, so I want the most affluent streets first."

"Hmm," said Emma. "Why do I feel like we're planning to rob a bank instead of carrying out a fund drive?"

However, when Melanie and Serena pointed out that she didn't have to participate if she didn't want to, she grumbled a bit but made no further objections. "Morgan is just being *practical*," they said. "She is absolutely right."

We decided that Brett should drive, as he owned a large minivan appropriate for the task. He had been paying little attention to our discussion, occupied as he was with shoveling huge amounts of meatloaf and mashed potatoes into his mouth with the mindless concentration of a backhoe digging a foundation, and, in his spare moments, waving at a brunette in a pink sweater at another table. He was therefore unaware that he had been elected to provide the transportation, until Melanie joggled his elbow.

"What?" he said. "Okay, I guess. But Helena will expect to come too." He made us a present of one of his huge smiles. "I can't drive you beautiful young women around without a chaperone."

"Helena is his *girlfriend*," Emma informed me. She seemed determined to drive a wedge between me and Brett. I had already figured out that the pink-sweatered girl believed herself to have some claims on him, but I felt certain I could pry him away from her, given half a chance.

Helena was one of the elite, a glossy creature from a fashion website. She stared at us with unbelieving eyes as we piled into the back two seats of Brett's car the next Saturday. She leaned over and whispered something into his ear as he turned the key in the ignition, and he laughed. The back two seats listened in resentful silence.

Once we arrived at our target neighborhood and the girls started fanning out to tackle different sections, I thrust a collecting can at Helena.

"Here," I said. "I know you'll want to help Brett, so—" I pointed to the far end of the street. "You can start all the way down there at the corner and work your way back."

Her eyes widened. "Me? I wasn't planning—"

"You're a senior, aren't you?" I asked. She nodded. "Have you got your volunteer hours completed?"

Her perfectly made-up face grew sullen. "No," she admitted.

I went on smiling and holding out the collecting can. After a pause she took it.

"Brett," she said, raising her voice, "you have to come with me. I'm not doing this alone."

"I'm sorry," I said. "We have to optimize our little team. No doubling up. Anyway," I added as she began to look mutinous, "you are both such great draws, it would be a shame to waste either of you."

She cocked her head, not understanding.

"Oh, I just mean that Brett is a basketball star, and you, of course, are totally *gorgeous*," I said. "Naturally anybody would want to give either of *you* a donation. Go up there and sell them on the basketball team! Make them understand why we need money for new uniforms! I'm sure you can do it if you try."

"Oh." She nodded as if this made perfect sense. "Okay, I suppose. Yeah," she said thoughtfully. "I imagine I could, if I tried."

I lowered my voice. "If there're any guys home, they're the ones for you to go after. I mean, what guy wouldn't be happy to give, when *you're* asking them? Know what I mean?"

She actually returned my wink, and sashayed down the road with her collecting can front and center.

I had reserved the finest, richest hunting grounds for myself. As the last of my team dispersed, I removed from the van a small bag I'd brought along and fished around inside it. *Let me see. . . .*

I slicked my newly shorn hair back with gel and secured it to my head with a tightly bound scarf. Examining myself in a compact mirror, I rubbed a little blue shadow under my eyes and cheekbones and then powdered my face to a sepulchral pallor. My collecting can was labeled with a bland, unspecific agency name. Satisfied, I approached my first house.

"Collecting for cancer? Oh dear, I suppose so," sighed the lady at the door. "Hang on a minute, let me get my purse."

I sagged suddenly against the screen door. "Sorry—so sorry! I'm just a little dizzy," I said.

"Oh, wow! Here, you'd better come in. Are you all right? Sit down, and I'll get you something to drink." She deposited me in a chair in her front hall, examining me with a heightened attention as she noted my pale skin and apparently hairless head.

"I'm fine," I said bravely as she disappeared down the hall toward the back regions. I leaned my head against the wall and rested my hands, palms upward, on my knees. When I heard her padding steps returning, I collapsed like a rag doll.

I timed it exactly. She walked in and looked at me, and for a split second I was bent over and breathing shallowly. Then, apparently becoming aware of her presence, I jerked to attention. I pasted a sickly smile on my face and sat up.

"Oh, thank you! You are so kind." I took the glass of water from her and drank greedily. I sighed and closed my eyes for a moment. When I opened them, I said, "I shouldn't bother you anymore. Thank you. I'll be fine now."

"No, indeed," she said. "You're not well. What agency are you working with? They ought never to have sent you out like this!"

"Oh no, honestly," I protested, "I'm fine, really I am! It was my idea to come out today. Look, there's the van, down the road. They'd be horrified. *Please* don't tell them. This is so embarrassing! Promise me you won't tell them. See, I feel much better already." I demonstrated, sitting up tall and smiling.

"Well . . . I suppose. You do look better. But you ought to take better care of yourself! Oh, that's right, you were collecting for . . . er, for—"

"It's a general fund, ma'am, for people suffering from cancer—to defray costs getting to the hospital for treatments, and so on. Any small amount will be appreciated."

"Oh yes, of course. I have my purse right here. Let me see, will fifty dollars be enough?"

Half an hour later I had received three hundred dollars, four glasses of water, and a shot-glassful of brandy. One heavily shawled and turbaned lady gave me twenty dollars. She whipped off her turban to show a bald head. "I've got small cell carcinoma. What have *you* got?"

Never missing a beat, I said, "Oh, I prefer not to discuss it. Sorry, but I'm not comfortable." I smiled wanly. "*You* look great, though. I hope you're getting better."

"Don't ever smoke cigarettes, kid," she said. "Don't *do* it."

"I won't," I said.

"Good. No, I suppose you wouldn't. Looks like you got your own problems." She seemed to want to move on to a detailed discussion of her prognosis, chemotherapy treatments, and doctor visits, so I made my excuses and was about to leave when she shot out a cold, clammy hand and grabbed my arm.

I don't like being touched by strangers, especially not a sick one. I pulled away. Her face got all mean and slitty-eyed, and she snatched the twenty-dollar bill right out of my hand. I was about ready to haul off and punch her one, when she pointed at my head.

"Next time," she said, "you'd better tuck *all* your hair under the scarf. Now get out of here and don't come back."

Uh-oh. I fingered the back of my neck. Sure enough, there was a wisp of blond hair that had escaped the scarf.

"Okay, no problem," I said, as easy as can be. I left, minus the twenty.

At that point it seemed like I ought to change my focus and switch back to actual charitable fund-raising, preferably a few streets away. This was a difficult moment for me, as I was doing so well, vacuuming tens and twenties and the occasional fifty up and down the street and tucking them into my pocket as soon as I was out of the direct line of sight of the donor. One part of my brain urged me to quit while I was ahead. Besides the ill will of Ms. Small Cell Carcinoma, what would my fellow volunteers think if I returned to the minivan with nothing to show for my afternoon? My status as a fund-raiser would surely drop like a rock, and my popularity would drop with it. Another part of my brain said, *Oh, c'mon! Just one more house for me!*

Luckily, I spotted Emma walking down the road. If

she were to see me made up like this she would notice, and the cancer lady might tell people about me. I raced to the van, removing the scarf and wiping my face and scalp with a moistened towelette. I grabbed a box I had brought along for food pantry items and cut through somebody's backyard to the street beyond so I'd be out of view of the sicko.

Lugging jars of peanut butter and tuna fish around was nowhere near as much fun, but at least I did get a respectable haul, using my acting and improvisational skills to wheedle big fat checks out of some of the house-holders. And a few, of course, did hand out cash, which automatically belonged to me, or at least, that's the way I figured it.

Rather to my irritation I discovered that the wealthiest households were *not* necessarily the most generous donors. A few of the richest ones tried to fob me off with a dollar. I accepted these offerings with teary-eyed gratitude, all the while allowing my gaze to wander over the Porsche in the driveway, the Persian rugs, the wide-screen TV, and the fancy antiques. Sometimes this did the trick, sometimes not. There are people out there who have *no* compassion for the disadvantaged.

When I returned to the van with my last box of food, it was packed with donations. My fellow philanthropists were growing tired; we had made a good-size haul for each of the causes, and everyone was feeling much more satisfied and companionable with one another than we had earlier.

We dropped off the food and checks for the food pantry and then went out for pizza. I managed to sit next to Brett. We talked about reverse lay-ups and left-handed dunks, which apparently have something to do with basketball, and he asked me to come watch him play at the gym after school on Monday. Helena missed this, as she was holding forth to Brooke about the pathetic sum—$27.45—that was the result of her afternoon's efforts. Even the pizza was the way I like it, with lots of meat and no vegetables. And when we paid, everybody else put in six dollars. I slipped my contribution in under the pile—three dollars folded so they looked like six dollars, sticking out from beneath the others. It was just a *little* scam after the major maneuvers of the afternoon, but it put the cherry on the top of the cake for me.

All in all, a good day. I felt something that might even have been a glow of liking for my companions.

11

ON SUNDAY, BROOKE'S GRANDMOTHER STOP–
ped by. She looked older than grandmothers in Los
Angeles generally do, which I assumed was because
she didn't dye her hair or go to the gym too much.
Actually, neither do some of the *abuelas* in my
neighborhood, but non-Hispanic white women in
Southern California tend to resent the encroach-
ments of old age and invest a lot of time in fighting
back.

We were all five seated cozily around the breakfast
table with a pot of tea and a plate of cookies, exchang-
ing family news, when it occurred to me how lucky I
was. When a woman that Brooke greeted as "Granny"
had walked through the door, I hadn't thought of the

possibility that it might have been her *paternal* grandmother, who would presumably have been *my* grandmother as well. Neither of my real grandmothers has ever been especially interested in me, but I understand that some grandmothers spend their golden years doting upon their offspring's offspring, demanding regular visits and photographs and so on. In that case the gig might have been up.

Luckily, this woman was apparently Aunt Antonia's mother, so all was well. Really, it was good that any other possibility had not occurred to me—my air of unconcern was perfectly natural.

"How are your parents, Janelle?" she asked.

I corrected her use of my name and then explained about the problem with my father's job that had cropped up in Brazil, and how my mother had closed the shop (what kind of shop? I wondered) and joined him in the swamp for three months.

"What kind of shop does your mother have, dear?" the nosey old thing wanted to know. "I would think that the fall would be a busy time for many businesses, in the lead-up to the holidays."

"Oh, she was speaking metaphorically, weren't you, Morgan?" said Aunt Antonia, smiling at me. "It's not really a shop."

I made a noncommittal noise and took a sip of tea, waiting for somebody else to fill Grandma in.

"Aunt Jackie is a real estate agent," said Brooke. *Thank you, Brooke.*

"And quite the go-getter," said her brother, Uncle Karl. "But the fall and winter are slow times. If Jackie and John are going to take a vacation, they usually do it around then. She knows a few young, hungry agents who are happy to take any calls she does get."

John, Jackie, and Janelle Johanssen? Were these people *crazy?* No *wonder* I wanted to change my name.

Grandma then began cross-examining me about the boyfriend from whose embrace I had been so cruelly torn. The other family members bit their lips and looked at one another out of the corners of their eyes, no doubt figuring I would burst into tears, or start throwing the cookies around the room at this tactless probing. I tried to remember what the guy's name was. Oh yeah. Ashton Something.

I folded my hands across one knee and responded, "I am doing well, thank you. I have put that behind me."

Brooke, her face scrunched up with the agony of recalling how Ashton had done me wrong with that blonde on Facebook, flung herself into the conversational fray. "Granny, guess what? I am learning to ride a horse. Morgan already knows how. She's so good that our instructor wants to train her to jump. Oh, and Morgan is a really, really wonderful fund-raiser for charities. You wouldn't believe how much she has gotten people to donate. She's absolutely brilliant!"

"My! It seems we have quite the highflyer in our family!" said Grandma. "Morgan, come over here beside me and tell me all about it."

So I got up and exchanged places with Brooke. Grandma went on quizzing me about my successes since I had blown into town three weeks before, and exclaiming in a gratifying manner over them. Finally I noticed that everyone else at the table had gone silent.

"Well, I shall have to come out to that stable and watch you, Morgan," Grandma said. "I'll be able to say I knew you when, after you go off to represent the USA on the Olympics jumping team."

Aunt Antonia cleared her throat. "Uh . . . Mother? Don't forget, *Brooke* is learning to ride too."

"Of course, of course." She looked around, trying to figure out where her actual grandchild had gotten to. "Brooke, of course! I'll go and watch *both* of you. How exciting for me!"

When she left, she pressed my hand and asked if I would like to come and visit her sometime.

"Sure," I said. I eyed the huge ruby solitaire rings on her knobby old hands. I'd be *happy* to pay a visit to Grandma's house, trust me!

The companionable feelings after the fund-raising day did not last. When I went to watch Brett play basketball after school on Monday, Helena attempted to physically remove me from the gym.

"What are *you* doing here?" she demanded.

"Brett asked me to come," I answered.

"Well, go away! You have no business here, you little out-of-town creep! I saw you smarming up to him last Saturday," she said. She gripped my arm with both hands and pushed me backward into the hallway. That was another difference between city and suburb—she had no idea how to fight. The girls at my old school would have twisted my arm behind me until I yelled, and marched me out of there, but Helena just did a bit of ineffectual shoving, expecting the simple fact of her aggression to defeat me.

"I only want to watch basketball practice," I objected. I swerved around and got past her, worming my way back into the room, with her still attached to my elbow. People were beginning to look at us, so she dropped my arm. "Brett *asked* me to," I repeated.

Helena pursued me to my seat on the bleachers, hissing like a teakettle on the boil.

"Who do you think you are, anyway?" she demanded in an angry whisper. "You just showed up out of nowhere, and now you're all over the place, sticking your finger into every pie. Brett is *my* boyfriend. Leave him alone."

"He's only your boyfriend as long as he wants to be," I said. "You can't lock him up, you know."

Red spots burned high on Helena's cheekbones. "Listen," she said. "I have lived here all my life. My friends and I *run* this school. Don't think that some little West Coast girl, a *junior*, no less, is going to sweep in here and grab my boyfriend. Not going to happen."

I studied her in silence for a moment. Actually, if only she knew it, I was a sophomore.

"Okay," I said, and smiled. At that moment Brett looked up and saw me. I waved. "Hey! Hi, Brett! Gee," I said, turning back to Helena, "he looks great in those shorts, doesn't he?"

"*Ooooh!*" she said, looking like she wanted to hit me. Fortunately, one of her friends called her over, and she left, casting furious glances in my direction. When she rejoined her friends, she said something and then pointed in my direction. They looked at me.

I smiled and waved, all friendly and unconcerned. One of them started to wave back, then jerked her hand down and thrust it under her thigh. Helena turned around and gave her a mean look.

Brett scored. I stood up and cheered. "*Yay, Brett!*"

Here is something I have learned: the best victim is somebody that nobody likes much, somebody that other people think *deserves* to be picked on. Bullies are fair game, for instance. Nobody feels sorry for them, and *I* become a heroine for teaching them a lesson. Even though Helena was one of the popular girls, I suspected that she was more feared than loved. If I toppled her from her position as Queen Bee of Lebanon Hill High, there would be no lasting animosity toward me, except, of course, from the ex-queen herself. So, as secure as she seemed, she was actually vulnerable.

She might not have been one of the cold like me—the cold at Lebanon were mostly males, and mostly engaged in a monotonous career of stealing cars and ditching them and then getting arrested for it, as well as one low-IQ sophomore girl who didn't seem to get the idea that there are cameras *everywhere* in stores these days—but Helena was a lot more like me than she was like whatever Brooke was. I understood Helena and what made her tick.

On the other hand, I did *not* understand Brooke. She was so open to being taken advantage of, so easy to fool, so generous and unguarded. Yet she wasn't stupid. It was more like she was *willing* herself not to see evil in the world, rather than being unable to do so. It would have been easy to victimize Brooke. She had no defenses, no idea that she could be in any danger. Yet I was wary of hurting her. I had the sense that any damage I caused her could boomerang around and smack me from behind. So, mentally, I declared Brooke off-limits.

Still, I *am* a creature of impulse, and Brooke might as well have been walking around with a big target painted on her back.

Our fund-raising efforts had pretty well exhausted the richer neighborhoods around Albany by the end of September. My hometown is a city of three or four million, while Albany doesn't even have a population of a hundred thousand. If you drive north up I-87, you get to Clifton Park, which is a good-size suburb, and a little further up the freeway is Saratoga, where the thoroughbreds race in the summertime and the affluent come to spend money. When I suggested we harvest these fertile fields, however, my partners in philanthropy objected.

"They'll want to give to their own food pantries," said Emma. "People like to see donated money go to help local causes."

Well, of course we didn't have to *tell* them that the money wasn't for their own food pantry, did we? However, this suggestion wouldn't play well with Straight-Arrow Emma.

There were lots of middle- and lower-class neighborhoods we hadn't touched, and I remembered how much more generous some of the people in the small houses were than some of the ones in the mansions. Still, I was getting bored with the door-to-door work, though it had been *very* profitable, for me and the *other* good causes.

I was ready for new worlds to conquer.

I was plenty busy. Academics were a stretch for me

still, so I spent hours on math and English. Luckily, Brooke was always ready to tutor me, so I was passing quizzes and contributing in class. We took the PSATs one Saturday too, which meant we had to miss a riding lesson. Brooke tied herself into knots over her performance on the test, but I breezed through. Who knew if I would be here when we got the results?

Back in early September, Helena had been premature in saying I had a finger in every pie. But by early October she was quite correct. I had infiltrated every organization of any importance at Lebanon Hill High. I was on the yearbook staff, the spirit week committee, the booster club team, and I was auditioning for the lead in *The Glass Menagerie*. The charity work is what gave me an in; I guess ambitious society ladies work the charity routine for the same reason. I was known and respected by staff and students alike, and welcomed into positions of influence and authority.

I kept my cash in Janelle's pink suitcase, and the pile was growing. In fact, I realized that I was going to have to exchange some of the fives and tens for larger denominations—it was getting a bit bulky. One day when I was secreting a new bundle of money, Mrs. Barnes walked into my room unannounced with a supply of fresh towels. I slammed the lid down the second I saw her out of the corner of one eye, but several bills fluttered out onto the floor.

"Oops!" I said gaily, gathering them up. "Look at me, throwing my money around!"

"You want to be careful about that," replied Mrs. Barnes, her face unreadable. She put the towels in the bathroom and then paused on her way out of my room. "There's a lot of money in this house," she observed. "Not that Mrs. Styles and Brooke care much about it. They're good people, for all they're so wealthy."

"They are," I agreed. "And they sure have been nice to me."

"Yes, they have," she said, and left, closing the door behind her.

Hmm. What was that all about? I was almost certain she hadn't seen anything but the twenty and the ten that had fallen out. I resolved to keep the pink suitcase locked from now on. And perhaps to pull a chair in front of the door when the suitcase was out and open.

Anyway, as I was saying, the money was mounting up, though I couldn't help but think with mingled frustration and resentment of the much larger sums I had been forced to hand over. After all, *I'd* done the work. Why should the charities reap such rewards? At least the net results were positive, and I was learning new skills all the time.

For instance, I was becoming more social. Back in my old school I'd been nobody. The power structure had firmed up in middle school, with me on the outside looking in. Now, coming here as an unknown entity from exotic Southern California, I had made a big splash in the small pool of Lebanon Hill High. I was reading people's faces and actions better these days, since there were so many who were not only willing but eager to talk to me. I was steadily hauling Brett into my orbit and out of Helena's, much to her chagrin. And I had discovered that whenever you are at a loss for what to do or say, if you put a pleasant, amused expression on your face and wait, like when Grandma wanted to know about my mother's shop, somebody will fill in the silence and fix the problem.

If I'd known what a great hustle this philanthropy stuff was, I'd have taken it up long ago. Then my parents might have been fooled into thinking I was a person of sterling character, and I wouldn't have had to leave home.

But if I hadn't left home, I might never have learned to ride, which I was enjoying more and more as Bounce allowed me to gallop all over her property, and I would almost certainly never have eaten Mrs. Barnes's pecan pie, one of the highlights of my life so far.

I had no complaints.

12

"AND NOW WE COME TO THE CHARACTER OF Morgan le Fay. An enchantress and a sorceress, she came of fairy blood, hence her name, 'le Fay,' which means 'of the fairies.' Morgan? Perhaps you can give us some insight into the character of your namesake?"

Ms. Tavernier, my English teacher, was trolling for comments during the last class of the day, at the peak of a long, golden October afternoon. The whole class was staring out the windows at blue skies and red and yellow foliage, bending their united will onto the clock on the wall to make it tick faster toward dismissal time.

I had finished reading "Sir Gawain and the Green Knight" the night before. It's this long medieval poem with somebody in it named Morgan le Fay. My interest was aroused by the name, so I did some research on her. Hers was an arresting and provocative personality, like mine.

"Fairies, or the fay, aren't those stupid little twits with wings in children's books," I responded. "They're like normal people, only much, much better. They're better-looking, smarter, and immortal. They can cast a spell of glamour so you don't see them as they actually are, and they can manipulate language so you'll believe anything they say. They're pretty amazing, and Morgan le Fay was their queen. *She's* the one who made the Green Knight and Sir Gawain do all that stuff in the poem. She was the one with the power."

Ms. Tavernier's eyebrows rose. I think maybe she had been almost as desperate to escape the classroom as the rest of us—her eyes had been flicking toward her watch—and hadn't expected much by way of a reply other than a shrug.

"Well, that was a spirited defense, Morgan! I don't believe I've ever seen you so animated before. You know, the fay are thought of as easily offended, malicious, and even cruel when annoyed."

"Of course," I agreed. "I mean, if you were dealing with inferiors, wouldn't you be kind of cranky if they weren't properly respectful?"

"Ummm . . ." A sharp crease formed between Ms. Tavernier's eyes. "I don't know about that—"

"Sure you would," I argued, because of course anybody *would*; she just didn't want to admit it. "And look, I know that the fay weren't great to mortals, but that's because they thought of humans the way that humans think of a domestic animal, that's all. You wouldn't get upset if the owner of a dog or a horse bred them and sold their offspring, would you? You wouldn't see anything wrong with training an animal to do a job for you."

Ms. Tavernier looked dazed. She opened her mouth to reply, but at that moment the bell rang and everybody surged to their feet. They rushed past me, a few of them casting dubious glances in my direction. I ignored them.

There were so many similarities between the cold and the fay! So yeah, okay, most of the cold I'd met in my life were pretty unimpressive, unlike the fairies of legend, but it only stood to reason that there would be dumb ones and smart ones, and that the smart ones (like me!) managed to hide themselves so you couldn't spot them.

I was enchanted with the fay.

I had set up in-store donation boxes (constructed by my little team of do-gooders, from cardboard and clear plastic) all over town, and the emptying of these had largely replaced the weekly door-to-door fundraising. These were tempting for me, as most of the contributions were in cash. I had to force myself to turn over the majority of the funds, or else people would get suspicious. Because you could *see* there was money in them. Another defect was that, as the boxes lacked my persuasive, in-person skills, they were not nearly so productive. Although I had no desire to go back to the hard slog of door-to-door, I was getting restless. I needed a better source of income.

And what do you know? V*oila!* A better source of income appeared.

The whole racehorse thing was Bounce's idea, not mine. Brooke was blathering on about our charitable activities while we were saddling up one Saturday.

"So you don't stick to one charity?" Bounce asked.

"No, Morgan says that there are so many deserving causes—it wouldn't be fair," Brooke said.

Yes, Morgan *had* said that, but actually, mixing it up meant that none of the charities would begin to feel proprietary about us, and hence likely to investigate too closely.

"I wonder, then . . . ," said Bounce.

Apparently Bounce's sister ran a horse rescue operation on a farm ten miles away, called Pegasus Stables. She took in retired thoroughbreds from the racetracks and tried to retrain and place them with new owners. If she couldn't, she kept them herself. Most racehorses retire before they're six, Bounce said, and then can go on to live another twenty or more years.

See, once horses stopped being used for transportation in the twentieth century, we didn't *need* them anymore. So, unless racehorses were big winners at the track, they were sold for slaughter and turned into pet food as soon as their competition days were over. Seemed perfectly sensible to me. Who needs some old slowpoke horse loafing around the place and eating its head off when there are races to be won? However, neither Brooke nor Bounce agreed with my (unspoken) opinion.

"Oh, how horrible!"

"Yes, after nearly killing themselves trying to please their owners, they were sold off for a few hundred dollars to be butchered. Perfectly healthy, young horses, some with scores of wins to their names. There's a new law against it in this country, but they still get sold to Canadian and Mexican dealers, who truck them back to their home countries and kill them there."

Brooke moaned in distress at this hard-hearted behavior.

"My sister's farm is an accredited not-for-profit organization," Bounce went on, "and I've always wanted to raise some money for her. You wouldn't believe how much one visit from the veterinarian can cost. Maybe we could use my stables . . . sell pony rides, or something? My expenses are high too, so I can't offer too much, but maybe you girls can think of a way."

"Ask Morgan," said Brooke, with touching faith. "She'll know what to do."

"Let me think about it," I said.

AFTER THE RACE IS RUN . . .

SADDLE UP AND ENJOY A DAY AT TWO AREA HORSE FARMS! FUNDS RAISED WILL BENEFIT RETIRED RACEHORSES

SATURDAY, OCTOBER 23RD
Rain Date, October 30TH

After the race is run, after the cheering dies down and the crowd goes home, after a racehorse's running career is over—[blah, blah. Lots of stuff here about poor old racehorses].

The junior class of Lebanon Hill High School is proud to sponsor this event to raise money to benefit Pegasus Stables in their work to help provide new lives for animals formerly in the racing industry.

We had to really scramble to get ready in time, but we had sponsors and volunteers standing in line for the chance to participate. You'd think everybody had been waiting all their lives to aid retired racehorses or something. I mean, what about the poor little doggies and kitty cats being done out of a square meal? Didn't anybody care about them not getting any horse meat to eat? It made no sense to me. Don't get me wrong—I enjoy riding, but once an animal outlives its usefulness, I'm not sentimental. I did get some idea of why this event was so popular, from Brooke's father, who thought it was a nice, "cultural" cause for his daughter to be involved in. Meaning, I guess, that it smelled of old, established money, and that definitely appealed to a car salesman. I had no difficulty signing Uncle Karl up as a major sponsor.

Albany is kind of worthy but dull. Pretty much its major purpose is as a place for legislators to gather and state workers to put in their forty hours a week until retirement age. But thirty-five miles north is the summer resort of Saratoga Springs, where the rich people go to gamble. Identifying with that sophisticated, glitzy world was a winning strategy.

And of course there were lots of juniors and seniors at school who needed to put in their volunteer hours and hadn't gotten around to it yet. As the committee chair, I used my power to give my own classmates preference, saying that this was a special junior class effort.

Besides making me popular with my fellow juniors, it had the extra advantage of irritating Helena, a senior, who had had her heart set on running the fancy hat contest. Sophomores and freshmen were restricted to tasks like following the horses around and doing poop-pickup duty.

Because the weather in this part of the world tends to turn pretty grim after Halloween, we were under pressure to complete our preparations quite quickly. Brooke, Emma, and Melanie served capably as my immediate underlings, churning out publicity, organizing volunteers, and coaxing donations of goods and services out of their nearest and dearest. When Brett realized that the event would not take place in a gymnasium and that there were no bouncy orange balls involved, he lost focus and wandered off to practice layups, and I didn't see much of him. Honestly, sometimes I wondered if I shouldn't let Helena just have him.

I, naturally, was in charge of finances.

I must confess that Brooke was invaluable to me. She shouldered boring and petty tasks without complaint and remained cheerful, however tense things got. It was a huge undertaking, and the fact that we had so many people helping meant that somebody had to schedule them and tell them what to do. Brooke was ever ready to jump into the Miata and fly off to fetch or carry or run the multitude of errands that needed to be done. The weather stayed beautiful and warm, so she flew from place to place like a jaunty little bird, with the top down and her hair flying in the breeze.

And this brings up the sole point of contention between us during the months when I lived with her family. Since I already had my driver's permit, I had been allowed to drive Aunt Antonia's Cadillac on several occasions, with a duly licensed driver in the passenger's seat. Although I was frequently told off for excessive speed, tailgating, and reckless overtaking, even Brooke and Aunt Antonia had to admit that I was both skillful and confident. Uncle Karl—who, by the way, owned a dashing little red Corvette he kept entirely for his own use—thought I was a hoot.

"And there she goes! Danica Morgan Patrick, moving up to the head of the pack! She cuts them off! She's in the lead!" he would yell.

"It's because you learned to drive in Los Angeles traffic, I suppose," Aunt Antonia said. "But really, Morgan, there is no need to be so aggressive here in upstate New York."

Yet no matter how well I drove, Brooke refused to teach me how to drive stick shift. When I persisted in my pleading, she would turn red and drop her eyes and then make some excuse to leave the room. I teased and begged and praised her little car, all to no avail.

She would not turn over the keys to the Miata to me, the selfish beast.

13

I PRETTY MUCH DITCHED SCHOOL WHILE WE prepared for After the Race Is Run. I mean, who had time for class when there were so many people to order around? Actually, my teachers cut me a lot of slack. I was raising money for some moldy old race-horses, which I guess trumped statistics and the Civil War in their minds. I guess it helped that our principal was an avid rider and a polo player and was going to ride in the demonstration. He was superhyped about the whole event and kept patting me on the back every time he saw me in the halls.

"Fine job, fine job, Ms. Johanssen! We're very proud to have you as a student here at Lebanon Hill High!"

And so they ought to have been. I am really, really

good, I was discovering, at organizing events. I admit I had a solid team to trot around behind me tending to the boring details. Brooke was everywhere, doing everything. Emma knew the horse world and had been in shows before, so that was helpful—she kept me from looking ignorant by jumping in with information, and all I had to do was keep my mouth shut. Melanie organized the decorations and designed posters and flyers.

Serena, being an animal lover, was naturally in seventh heaven and had to be forcibly removed from the horse barns because otherwise she wasted her time petting and cooing over them. She braided their tails and manes with satin bows, securing them with flower scrunchies and putting stupid hats with ear cutouts on their heads. She was lucky not to get kicked, in my opinion—they looked ridiculous. I stopped her before she got to *my* horse, physically barring her entry into Chessie's stall.

"No," I said.

She protested but gave in, daunted by the look in my eye. "I've signed up for riding classes too, so I'll be joining you on Saturday mornings in the future," she said.

Fine. She and Brooke could lurch around the baby ring together and dress their horses up in pink tutus, for all I cared, so long as they left me to practice in peace. I, of course, was to demonstrate jumping at the benefit, along with Bounce's niece and her friends.

During the course of planning After the Race Is Run, I had to fill out a lot of documents and forms, and eventually, as I was in and out so often, I got the run of the high school office files. I am sorry to say that it didn't occur to me immediately to take advantage of this fact. It was only after I ran across my own student file with a copy of my birth certificate, social security number, school transcript from LA, current grades and reports and so on, that I realized what a treasure trove this was. I copied everything (and a few other files for good measure) and brought them back home with me, secreting the pile of papers underneath my mattress for later study and consideration.

I might not be any Michelangelo, but I felt certain that, with a little practice, I could learn to fake documents.

The day before the event I had a big crew swarming over Hidden Hollow Ranch. There was less to do at Pegasus Stables because Bounce's sister was handling that. Some stuff had to wait until the next morning, but we were organizing so that we had as little as possible to do at the last minute.

One member of the crew of volunteers was the stupid cold girl who kept getting caught stealing at the mall. She was trailing around the stables, not doing much work and projecting a general aura of deceit and untrustworthiness. She ran her greedy little fingers over everything—pitchforks, dung shovels, bags of bran, saddles, and tack, assessing possible salability and cash potential.

"Watch out for old light-fingered Francea over there," I said to Brooke and Emma in a low tone. "I'm not sure what she thinks she's going to steal from a stable, but I'm sure she'll find something."

"What do you mean? Why would she steal something?" asked Emma, as Brooke stared at me, open-mouthed.

Evidently Francea had come to the same conclusion about there not being much worthwhile to steal in a barn, because she began drifting away, toward the parked cars. She started walking oh-so-casually up and down the rows of vehicles, casting glances in through the windows, looking for any unprotected valuables that might be ripe for the picking.

"Because," I said, checking off the latest task on my list, "it is her nature to steal, that's why. She eats, she sleeps, she steals. Francea the Felon. Didn't you know? She's been barred from every shopping mall in a thirty-mile radius. One more conviction, and it's off to reform school."

They both turned to look at Francea, disbelieving. I could not imagine how they did not know this. She might as well have been wearing a T-shirt labeled, I AM A THIEF.

"Stop staring, and we'll catch her in the act. Even

Francea isn't stupid enough to take something while you're looking right at her."

They stopped, but only so that they could begin arguing in loud whispers.

"If that's true, I don't *want* to catch her in the act. The poor girl!" cried Brooke.

"I don't know," said Emma. "It might be better if she does get caught. Then she could get some counseling. Wow, she must have some real trauma in her background to act like that."

I stopped running my eyes down the list of chores and looked at them.

"Why do you think that, Emma?" I asked. "And why do you feel sorry for her, Brooke?" Honestly, I was curious. Why would they react like that? "Your cars are both parked out there. Did you leave anything in them you'd regret losing? Doesn't it make you mad to think of her taking your stuff?"

They both turned to see how close Francea was to their cars. Not too close, evidently, because they turned back again.

"Everybody knows that people steal compulsively like that because they're compensating for some deep-seated loss in their life," Emma said. "It's hardly even her fault. She should be stopped because it isn't fair to the rest of us, but she needs counseling so she can make her peace with whatever bad experiences are making her do this."

"Oh, I suppose you're right," Brooke said. "I just hate to see people cornered and caught. It's like watching one of those nature shows where the predator is stalking its prey. I can't look; I can't even stand thinking about it." She shuddered.

Huh. I kind of like those shows.

"What if she steals because she enjoys stealing?" I asked. "What if she's had a perfectly normal childhood but happens to think it's more fun to take things than it is to save up money to buy them?"

Emma shook her head pityingly. "You are taking a very old-fashioned view of crime. Nobody is born evil. Nobody is born a thief. People don't do terrible things without reason. Nope, she's compensating for something."

"And you say she's been caught before," said Brooke. "Now that she knows the consequences, why would she keep doing it if she weren't driven to it?"

Consulting my own personal experience, I offered some suggestions: "Poor impulse control? Thrill seeking? A taste for the finer things in life coupled with a disinclination to pay for them?"

They both smiled at me and shook their heads.

Okay, if you say so. Far be it from *me* to disillusion you.

"Say, isn't that your mother's Subaru, Emma?" I inquired. "You know, the one whose glove box Francea has her hand in right now?"

Emma snapped to attention. *"What?"*

"That looks like a fine set of binoculars she's secreting in that big handbag of hers," I added.

She gasped. "Those are my dad's Vortex Razor! He'll kill me if those get stolen. He always tells me to lock the car, but I forgot they were in there."

"What do we do?" whispered Brooke.

"We get them back!" said Emma. She set her jaw and looked like she was about to march over to Francea and shake them out of her.

"But how? Won't she deny it if we ask her?" Brooke restrained Emma by clutching her arm. "Oh, Morgan, what should we do?"

"I'll get them," I said. "But if I do, you both owe me. Stay here and don't move."

Not pausing to see if they agreed with this proposition, I began walking fast in Francea's direction. Alarmed, she veered away from the Subaru and moved several cars away. Once she was screened by a big van, she faked a sudden need to retie her shoe and bent over.

While it was true that I could not see her, it was also true that she could not see me. I walked softly around the back of the van and up behind her. I grabbed the big handbag.

"Eeek!" Francea whirled around. "What . . . what are you doing?"

I turned and checked to make sure we were out of the

line of sight of Emma and Brooke. We were. I rummaged through the bag and found the binoculars. I slipped the strap around my neck and kept rummaging. Four cell phones, a tablet computer, a wad of cash, several credit cards with a variety of different people's names, and a bottle of vodka. Oh, and a tiny little handgun.

"That's mine!" Francea cried as I brandished the last item.

"Oh? I thought it might belong to your kid brother. It looks like a toy."

Her eyes shifted frantically back and forth, considering this opening. She was too young to have a license for it, and we both knew it.

"It . . . yes, it is a toy. It's my brother's, like you said. Can I have it back?"

"It sure is realistic," I said, tilting it to admire the light gleaming off the barrel. "Looks like it could do some damage, small as it is." I'd never handled a gun before, but I suspected that the little catch thing was the safety. I fiddled with it.

"No, it's just a—"

Bam! The bullet hit the ground by her right foot, and she leaped into the air like a prima ballerina. Yes, that was the safety, for sure.

"My goodness, how alarming. I thought you said this was your brother's toy." I aimed the little gun squarely at Francea.

"Keep it! Keep everything!" she gabbled. "Please don't shoot me."

"Really, Francea, you are an embarrassment to our tribe." I smiled and shook my head at her in pained disappointment.

"To our what?" She peered at me, trying to read my expression. "I'm sorry! I'll go straight. Honest. I'll never steal again."

"Uh-huh, sure."

"Don't you believe me?" To my mingled admiration and hilarity, two big tears streaked down her cheeks. This idiot actually thought that *I* would pity her "distress."

"No, I don't believe you, but I *am* impressed. Neat trick, those tears!"

"Yeah, well, um. So . . . can I go?"

"Sure. No, wait." She wavered, considering flight, but then thought better of it. The gun was still aimed at her. I found her wallet, examined the library card to ensure the wallet was hers, stripped it of cash (a tidy sum, by the way), and threw it to her. She caught it and stared at me, openmouthed.

"You're a *thief*!" she said in tones of righteous indignation. "You—you *stole* my money! You knew it was mine and you *took* it."

"Did you think you were the first person to come up with the idea? You don't have a patent on larceny. Now beat it," I growled. As she hurried off through the maze of cars and I stuffed the goodies back into the handbag, I smiled reminiscently. I remembered the carnie guy telling *me* to beat it all those years ago. Somehow I doubted that Francea would learn as much from this encounter as I had from him.

I stepped out from behind the van and found Brooke and Emma dodging around the cars, bent low but approaching cautiously. Lucky I hadn't delayed any longer, or they might have been in a position to overhear our final remarks.

"We called 911! Are you okay? Was that a gunshot?"

I showed them the little gun. Brooke gasped and threw her arms up in front of her face, like that would protect her from stray bullets.

"Oh, honestly, Brooke! I'm not going to shoot you. It went off accidentally. Look, I'm putting the safety on." I pointed the gun down at the ground and twiddled with the catch. With any luck it had been rendered harmless.

I told them the story of my ambushing Francea as she'd hid behind the van.

"I snuck up behind her and grabbed her purse," I said truthfully. Less truthfully, I continued, "And when I did, everything fell out. The gun went off—I guess when it hit the ground, or maybe I hit it with my hand. She tried to pick stuff up, but all she got was her wallet before she took off."

"Okay, look," I said, eying them sternly. "You called 911?"

They nodded. I could hear sirens coming nearer, now I thought of it.

"We are not going to tell them whose purse this is."

They both burst into confused, argumentative speech. I waited patiently for a break in the yammering.

"Tomorrow is After the Race Is Run, remember?"

They nodded. The sirens were entering the grounds of the ranch.

"Do you really think that they will let us go on with the program if they find out about Francea?" Actually, they probably would have. Why not? I just didn't want people possibly staying home because they'd read about Francea's arrest in connection with the festival and had gotten nervous. I continued to fix them both with an unrelenting stare.

"Maybe not," said Emma.

"Do you want all of our work to be ruined because of Francea? How about you, Brooke? You're the one who can't bear the idea of running to ground a fugitive from justice. Does either of you even know her last name or where she lives? I sure don't," I lied.

"I think it was fate that made her take her own wallet instead of any of the things she'd stolen," I continued, on a lofty note. "Well, that or maybe self-preservation, so the theft couldn't be linked to her. In any case, the cops won't know who she is if we don't tell them. Personally, I think that if we turn these things over to the police, we'll be doing the right thing." Naturally, I had already transferred the cash to my own pockets. "How about it? Here they come."

"But the gun!" Brooke protested.

"Oh, it's not hers! She found that, and figured she could sell it," I said.

Brooke and Emma looked at each other.

"I guess," said Brooke. "If you're okay with it, Emma."

"Yeah, I suppose."

The cops questioned me closely, which wasn't surprising, given the gun. I described Francea vaguely enough that she could be any of a dozen girls, but accurately enough that, if they figured out which one she was, it wouldn't sound like I had been trying to mislead them. I said that I couldn't be sure if she went to our school—considering as how I was new there this year.

They had to go through the whole crowd of people working there that day, getting names and trying to match the stolen items to the owners. I heard later that nobody claimed the gun, which appeared to be unlicensed. Somebody in this public-spirited crowd was being naughty.

The one thing that everybody—cops, volunteers, and

stable staff—agreed upon was that I was a truly remarkable young woman.

"So brave, so strong," said my cousin Brooke. "Really," she said, when her parents and grandmother showed up to escort us home, "I've never met anyone like her in my life."

14

EVERYONE IN THE HOUSEHOLD WAS INVOLVED in After the Race Is Run, even Mrs. Barnes, the housekeeper, who was one of the breakfast cooks. We were therefore up at dawn on the day of the benefit, and over at the stables setting up by seven. At ten thirty, when the event was already in full swing and crowds of people were wandering around, I realized that I had left some of the paperwork I needed back at the house, so Emma offered to run me back to pick it up.

When we got there, Emma waited in the car, as we both assumed I would be inside for less than a minute. I would have been too, except that the phone rang while I was passing through the hall on the way out, paperwork in hand.

Since I still had no cell phone, people had to reach me by using the house phone. It might, therefore, have been somebody calling about the event, with a message I needed to hear. I groaned but veered into Uncle Karl's study to pick up the handset.

"Styles residence," I said, seating myself behind Uncle Karl's desk. My eye roved over the papers laid out on the surface. Generally he was tidy, so his early start this morning must have distracted him from doing his filing. A letter from his lawyer, one from his accountant, and a few bills. Interesting. I had never thought of looking through his desk before, but a little exploration might pay off sometime in the near future.

A faraway voice floated up from the earpiece of the receiver.

"Hello? Hello, is that Brooke? This is Janelle. Your cousin from Los Angeles."

A small eternity seemed to pass. My brain finally kicked into gear. Janelle. From Los Angeles.

"Where are you?" I said at last.

"It's—oh, I'm at this little lake in the San Jacinto Mountains a few hours away from LA. Brooke, I am so, so sorry that I skipped out on coming to live with you guys. It's been awful. If I'd known what he was like—"

"Uh-huh," I said, rolling my eyes. Yeah, trust good old what's-his-name to screw up.

"You must have thought it was pretty weird when that other girl showed up instead of me."

"What other girl? There was no other girl," I said firmly. I wanted the girl she'd met at the airport kept entirely out of this conversation. "You simply weren't there when we went to get you. We were scared to death. What are you talking about?"

"Oh, right. So . . . okay, never mind her, then. But, see, I'm in awful trouble, Brooke. I haven't got any money and my boyfriend has, like, *deserted* me here all by myself without a car or anything. He left here headed for Las Vegas. I don't know what to do. I never should have ditched you like I did. I wish I was in Albany now instead of here. I never want to see Ashton again for the rest of my life." At this point she hiccupped and broke down into noisy tears.

Great. Every time I talked to this girl, she was sobbing.

Finally the storm subsided and I heard some broken murmurings, from which I picked out a few words.

"They must *hate* me! *Why* won't they answer me?"

"Who must hate you?" I inquired, not bothering to disguise my voice. She had convinced herself that I was Brooke, and seeing that the two girls hadn't spoken in years, how was she to know? She wasn't likely to remember the sound of *my* voice from that brief interlude in LAX.

"My *parents!*" Her voice became a little more controlled. "I keep calling and calling them, but they never pick up the phone and they never call me back! And there's no electricity here because Ashton's horrible uncle turned it off, and I can't charge my phone—it's this cheapo prepaid thing, anyway. And besides, there's no reception, so I have to walk three miles into this tiny little village to use a public phone. Can you believe it? They have a *pay* phone in the convenience store. It took, like, a *million* quarters to call New York. And Ashton is just *gone*, and he's not answering my phone calls. And I think I might be pregnant! And I *don't know what to do-hoo-hoo!*"

Lots of wailing on the other end of the phone.

While she howled, I thought fast. I had to decide. Should I hang up, go upstairs and pack, and then spin some sort of a tale so that Emma would drive me to the airport? I would take with me the files I had had the foresight to swipe. Once in a new location I could fake up some identification that made me look eighteen. Or, of course, I could go back to my parents and resume my position in their house.

No.

Not a chance. I had come too far, learned too much, gained too much power and influence here, to go back again. I *liked* it here. I *liked* my riding lessons. I *liked* eating Mrs. Barnes's cooking. I *liked* living in luxury.

I wanted the big event that *I* had envisioned and was bringing to reality today to be a huge success. I wanted to be hailed as the heroine of Lebanon Hill High, admired by one and all (except Helena). Okay, I probably wasn't going to be able to stay much longer—not unless I could somehow vaporize Janelle long-distance through the telephone—but I wanted a week or two more, at least.

"It's a good thing I'm the one who answered the phone, Janelle," I said in a low, confidential voice. "Yes, I'm afraid your parents are really mad at you. And so are mine. Pretty much everybody is. I overheard my parents talking about it. 'She's made her bed. Now let her lie in it.' That's what your mother said. Everybody assumed you took a bus or hitchhiked back to California to meet up with Ashton somewhere. Your mom was so pissed off that you'd scared us all like that—she said she didn't ever want to see you again. She thought you probably *would* get pregnant, and she said she'd be ashamed to be the grandmother of a baby born to a sixteen-year-old girl. I'm sorry to tell you this, but you have to understand the situation."

The scream of fury coming through the phone nearly cracked my eardrum.

"My mother *is such a bitch!*"

Actually, I had to agree. As brief as my exposure to her mother had been, I'd come to the identical conclusion.

"But look, are you sure you're pregnant?" I asked.

"Well . . . maybe not. We did use a, you know, a condom most of the time. I'm not due for my period for a while yet—I'm just scared I might be. Because then what? And they don't have any pregnancy test kits at the convenience store. I looked. It's super-rural around here, and I don't have a car."

"Oh, you can't tell with those home tests until you're two or three months along, anyway," I said. I had absolutely no idea if this was true or not. "Listen; here is what I think we should do. Can you stay where you are for a few weeks, until you're sure if you're . . . you know, expecting?"

"I haven't got any *money!*"

I sighed. This was going to be painful, but there was no help for it.

"I have some saved up," I said. "If I sent you, like, a few hundred dollars, could you make that last until you know for sure? Because I think I could talk my parents into paying for you to come out here like you were going to before. See, your parents are seriously ticked off. But *my* parents think that *your* parents are being too harsh. Only, it would really help if I could tell them that you're not pregnant."

"Oh." She thought about this for a moment. "That's nice of you. But maybe, if you sent me some money, I could go home. I mean, they couldn't actually kick me out."

"I wouldn't do that if I were you," I said. If she went home and found the house empty, she'd probably talk to the neighbors, or get in touch with one of her friends, and there was sure to be *some* way of contacting the Johanssens in Brazil. "See, your parents decided to go away on a little vacation, so they're not there. And before they left," I added, "they changed the locks on your house, so if you came home, you wouldn't be able to get in."

"*What?* What century are we living in, the Middle Ages? Lots of girls get pregnant! Okay, I can see they'd be mad, but they *changed the locks?*"

"I'm sorry, Janelle. Yeah, it does seem pretty mean, but that's what they told my mom and dad. Honestly, if you would just stay where you are for a week or two, until we know if there's anything to worry about, I think that would be best. If you aren't pregnant, I *might* even be able to get your parents to take you back," I added as one last inducement.

"Wow." She was silent a moment. "I'm not sure I even *want* to go back, if they're going to be that awful. I guess that explains why they never came looking for me. I kind of expected them to eventually figure out about Ashton's uncle's camp when they realized we were both missing. But, like, it's been *months* and they haven't even checked. That is so *cold*! I'm better off without them. Except . . . I'm only sixteen! I don't have a job, I don't have any money—"

"I'll send you some money," I said hastily. "I'll do it right away and Express Mail it to you. What's your address?"

After a bit more sobbing and wailing, I got an address and we arranged for her to call when she knew what her situation was. We hung up, and for a few seconds I sat there, thinking. It wouldn't buy me a whole lot of time, but at least I could finish up with After the Race Is Run, collect a bunch more money, and exit in a dignified and organized way, instead of fleeing with the police of two states on my trail.

Emma. She was going to be wondering what I was doing in here so long. Oh, well. I'd think of something. I always do.

I groaned aloud as I peeled off fifteen twenty dollar bills (fifteen!) and tucked them into an envelope, but it was a necessary sacrifice. I needed Janelle to stay put and stay quiet for a little while longer while I planned my future. I addressed the envelope, omitting Janelle's name for the moment so Emma wouldn't spot it. Then I went out and hopped into the car.

"I thought you must have slipped through a portal to another dimension or something," Emma said. "What took you so long?"

When in doubt, tell the truth. Or some of it.

"The phone rang and I answered. It was a relative of

ours." Well, of Brooke's, anyways. "She's in a jam because she needs her medication. She left it here by mistake, and she really needs it. So we have to make a superfast run to the post office and Express Mail it to her."

Emma rolled her eyes. "Right now, of all times? I have to say, Morgan, I think it's amazing how you can have this amount of responsibility on your shoulders, but you never seem to break a sweat. I'd probably be cursing her out right this second, but you don't even seem to mind."

"It'll be okay," I said. "But don't mention it to anybody, would you? No big deal, but nobody knows she was here at the house but me. She's having problems with her parents, and she wanted to talk. We'll make it back in time—we just have to *move*. C'mon, Emma, I bet this dumpy old station wagon can go a *lot* faster than this."

"I'm already doing forty! In a thirty-mile-an-hour zone!"

"Oooh! Scary! What a lawbreaker you are!"

"Okay, but if I get stopped, *you* can pay the fine." Rounding the corner at a death-defying forty-five miles an hour, Emma shrieked. She was a real daredevil, that one.

We had the money Express Mailed off to Janelle in no time, and nobody at Hidden Hollow even noticed how long it had taken us to fetch the papers. They were working steadily, changing soiled tablecloths, emptying trash bins, moving folding chairs from one place to another as our needs changed, rearranging flowers and plates of cookies, leading horses and ponies around.

It was a beautiful day. For the previous week everybody had studied the weather forecasts like they were the Delphic oracle or something. Not me. I figured it would either be nice or it wouldn't. As Emma had said, I don't break into a sweat over much of anything. In the long-range forecast there had been rain threatened for the day of the benefit, but gradually the storm warnings shifted off. We had clear skies and a big yellow sun. The peak of the autumn leaf season was past, but there was still plenty of color left, and, at least in the sunshine, the air was soft and warm.

I am not especially sensitive to pretty landscapes or fine artwork, and I am certainly not sentimental, but for a minute there I almost got it about how people didn't want to see these horses turned into Alpo.

Once we'd checked out the progress at Hidden Hollow, we took a quick drive over to Pegasus to see how the events were proceeding there. The horses were outside, and a nice-size crowd stood by the fence, watching them being put through their paces. They were like fine leather goods from Hermès, or maybe a classic car from Rolls-Royce: beautiful and classy and . . . I don't know, *expensive* looking. Like something I would be proud to own.

I watched them go by, shining in the sun, and, letting go of my usual caution, I said aloud what I was actually thinking. "I guess they *are* worth a certain amount of trouble."

Everybody, the Styles family, Emma, Melanie, Bounce, and Bounce's sister, burst out laughing. The sound was so loud and raucous that it startled the horses, and they shook their heads and whinnied. These people thought that what I'd said was a masterpiece of understatement, but of course it wasn't; it was a simple statement of fact, and quite a stretch for me, frankly. Normally the only thing I thought was worth this much effort was *me*.

But those horses were beautiful, desirable, valuable objects, and therefore worth trouble, and possibly even some of my hard-earned money, in order to protect and preserve them. I toyed with the idea of skimming off a smaller amount for myself and leaving a substantial sum to actually benefit the animals. It might be worth it, if only to prove to myself how much control I had over my acquisitive nature.

On the other hand, I wasn't likely to be around much longer to reap the benefits of having saved them from the canning factory. And there was no doubt I was going to need a lot of cash to make a new life for myself.

So, deal with it, horses. I'd decide about the extent of my generosity when the time came.

15

EVEN WITH MY HIGHLY DEVELOPED ABILITY TO delegate boring work to others, I was swamped all day at After the Race Is Run. However, since it was well known that I was the organizer and brain behind the event, I did not mind; I got so much praise and approval that I found myself almost literally purring with satisfaction.

Nearly everybody from school came, even Brett (*without* Helena). He looked around at the crowds of people happily eating sausages and pork roast, the ladies wearing floral dresses and hats shaped like birthday cakes and birds, the kids riding ponies in the ring and patting the velvety noses that protruded from every stall, and said, "Cool! But don't horses do anything more than walk around in a circle?"

The guy was an idiot. If I hadn't disliked Helena so much, I'd have told him to take a hike. And of course, he *was* awfully good-looking.

I told him to go and watch the jumping and polo demonstrations for some suggestions about what horses could do besides walk around in a circle. Then I had to leave, as I was scheduled to put Chessie through her paces and demonstrate how to get the most out of a horse in a jumping exhibition in front of an admiring audience.

"She's utterly fearless," I heard Bounce say proudly as I waited my turn to ride into the ring. "I've never had such a promising student before. And the bond she has with that horse is remarkable. I wouldn't have pegged Chessie as a jumper, but Morgan has convinced *Chessie* that she is. She simply lets the horse know what is expected, and the horse loves her so much that she does it."

Involuntarily I snorted. Chessie stiffened, raising her head to slew her eyes around at me, trying to judge my mood. She danced nervously. No, I didn't deceive myself for a moment that she obeyed because she loved me. I thought better of my Chessie's intelligence than that. The horse knew what was good for her, that's all. No big secret there.

By this time Chessie and I had learned each other so well that we moved as if we were one animal, click-

ing through the various paces as if we had been pro-
grammed, and soaring like a lark over any obstacle that
happened to be in our way.

I wondered if, after I had left upstate New York, I
should head to the hunt country in Virginia, where
I could pursue a fox over open fields, leaping fences
and ditches with wild abandon. That sounded like a lot
of fun, but I had been involved with horseback riding
long enough to know that it was an expensive hobby.
Still, I had skills now, and that might get me a job at
a stable. *Not* the equal of the position I enjoyed here,
but at least I'd have a chance to indulge in my time
off. I'd have to fudge up a letter of recommendation—I
couldn't exactly expect Bounce to write one after I'd
been exposed as an impostor and walked off with the
majority of the proceeds from this event.

Stupid Janelle. She was ruining everything.

One last jump, higher than any before. The crowd
held its collective breath, and then there were gasps of
pleasure and gratification as we sailed over and landed
gracefully on the other side. Applause ushered us out of
the ring. I smiled and touched my finger to the brim of
my hat in salute as we strode away.

I felt almost fond of Chessie in that moment.

There were other jumpers after me—Bounce's niece
and so on—but once I was finished, everybody else was
an anticlimax. I nodded at the other participants and

said random things like, "Nice job," and "You've got a good seat," because that was what was expected. They said, "Yikes, I wouldn't want to go up against *you* in a competition! We heard you were something special, and I guess so!"

I just smiled.

"Morgan! Morgan, did you see me? I didn't fall off or make a fool of myself or anything!"

It was Brooke, of course. I *hadn't* seen her, being far too busy to bother, but of course I lied and said I had.

"And Emma did great too. She's good. Not like you, of course, but better than me. Well, that wouldn't be hard, would it?"

No, it wouldn't, but I didn't say so.

"Girls, you both were wonderful!" The Styles family had come up to congratulate us. Uncle, Aunt, and Grandmother clustered around, admiring and happy. Aunt Antonia made a big fuss over Brooke in order to compensate for the fuss Uncle Karl and Grandma were making over me.

"Such grace! So cool and collected! You make it look so easy!" they said, rendered starry-eyed by their first view of my riding skills.

"Well, *Brooke* only started lessons in September," said Aunt Antonia, "so I think it's remarkable that she has learned enough to appear in public in an exhibition like this. Morgan has had years of practice. Though, of course," she amended, looking a little embarrassed at her own vehemence, "she certainly is impressive."

The truth was, as *you* know, that I had had no more practice than Brooke. I simply had the talent and she did not.

"Brooke has improved," I said.

To my surprise I saw a flare of anger in Aunt Antonia's eyes. She was opening her mouth to deliver what I thought would be a sharp reply, when Brooke forestalled her.

"Yes, I *have* improved, haven't I? I was so proud of myself," she said, and she *looked* proud of herself too. Weird. If I were her, I would hate my guts, knowing how inferior I was to me, if you follow what I'm saying. But Brooke seemed incapable of jealousy. It was actually a bit annoying.

I looked at Aunt Antonia to see how she would respond to this. What was biting the woman, anyway? I hadn't said anything mean. I'd been polite—gracious, even.

Aunt's face softened. She bent forward and kissed her daughter's forehead and stroked her hair. "And we are proud of both of you, but especially of *you*, Brooke, for learning so much so quickly." She looked around at her husband and mother, as though defying them to contradict this last statement.

They paid no attention but continued to pepper me with comments and questions. Well, of course. *That* was what was annoying Aunt. We were supposed to pretend that Brooke and I were equally worthy of praise.

At last Aunt Antonia grew so annoyed by the attention being showered on me instead of upon her beloved Brooke that she linked arms with the other two and carried them off, saying, "Come on! I want some ice cream, and these young ladies have a great deal of work ahead of them. It's a wonderful event, girls. Everybody is saying so. We'll see you later!"

It's funny. I was born not quite understanding the way most people think and, especially, feel. I have to study them to figure out how they will react to things I say or do. Yet in this situation Uncle Karl and Granny were being obtuse, while I totally got that Aunt Antonia was resenting my success. She didn't like everybody ignoring Brooke and concentrating on me. Okay, I didn't exactly know what it was in my words or tone that had ticked her off a minute before, but I knew why she was so ready to take offense.

But still, she was reluctant to demand that her mother and the father of her only child ignore me and heap praise on Brooke. This was where human relations got confusing for me. Aunt Antonia wanted her daughter to win. I understood this, although personally I can't imagine caring about anybody else's success but my own. Yet, for some reason that I did *not* understand, having to do with "morality," or "being a good person," she could not bring herself to say so or act on her feelings.

It must be complicated, being a person with a conscience.

In any case she was right. There was a lot of work ahead of us, and it kept coming at us hour after hour. I had the extra duty of siphoning off a good chunk of the cash for myself in an inconspicuous way. This was harder than you might think. Bounce kept *worrying* about the cash boxes. You'd have thought everybody attending was there for the express purpose of ripping us off.

As usual I ignored the checks and went for good old dollars. Twenties were my personal favorite—not so large that they were memorable, but much less bulky than ones. I was stashing my share of the loot into an inner breast pocket of my riding jacket, and I didn't want to start to look *too* much better endowed on one side than the other.

While planning the event, I had resisted the suggestion of my fellow committee members to procure tickets with numbers. I claimed that I did not want them because of the extra expense and the time crunch, but really it was so that nobody could compare the number of tickets sold and the amount of money in the cash boxes. This way I could manipulate the attendance numbers to suit my own purposes. Everybody knows that head counts based upon simple impressions are inaccurate.

Later in the day Francea showed up on a bicycle. I suppose she was on the lists as a volunteer, so she figured she had better at least make an appearance, and couldn't resist getting into an event for free. But when she spotted me, she got all shifty-eyed and slithered away, out toward the parked cars again. That girl didn't have an original thought in her head. There was nothing of mine out in the parking lot, so I didn't care. Later I saw her dragging a trash bag full of stuff away. She tried to jam it into the basket of her bicycle, but it was too big and things kept falling out onto the ground. People started looking curiously at her and her bag of stolen goods. Leaving half the fallen electronics and assorted goodies where they lay, she slowly wobbled away on her bike.

Fine, I thought. *Excellent. If anybody suspects there's any money missing, we will know who to blame—there were plenty of witnesses. Thank you, Francea.*

The sun slid downward toward the west. The crowds lessened a little, and I got a break to walk around like a paying customer. I stopped by the petting zoo and tried to figure out why these kids, and even some adults, were so anxious to feed and touch a bunch of alpacas and lambs and baby ducks. I guess they're soft and "cute"— whatever that is—but even baby animals can bite. I watched as one little boy got knocked over by a goat, greedy for the feeding bottle the kid held in his hand. How the boy howled!

A little further on there were snakes and lizards. Older kids were interested in these, but they bored me, the sluggish things. As I approached the hawks and owls, though, I perked up. Those sharp beaks and talons attracted me. Unlike the fluffy grass-and grain-eaters in the petting zoo, these were predators, swift and merciless. I wondered what would happen if I let one of them go. Would I enjoy watching it fly, seeing it pounce on a victim? The woman tending the birds was a falconer—she flew them in search of prey.

"Yes, I love it, but you have to go out in all weather: rain, shine, or snow. It takes real dedication. It's not for everybody," she was saying to a small crowd of onlookers.

Okay, not for me, then. I don't go out in bad weather for any reason, let alone to watch some dumb bird kill a mouse. I turned away.

"I might have known you'd be here, Morgan!"

"Hi, Brooke," I said. She was smiling, tired but happy and enjoying the day.

"I hardly remember anything about you from when we were little, but I do remember *that*," she said, nodding her head at the whole scene, with the sheep and the snakes and the owls.

"Remember what? Remember from when? We barely knew each other when we were kids." For some reason I was feeling irritable and jaded. I had no patience for this "remember when" stuff.

"Sure we did. It was a long time ago, and I don't recall a whole lot of details, but you came out here for a week once, oh, back when we were both about seven years old. We went to a petting zoo like this, remember?"

"No," I said. I was looking around, wondering if I should nip behind the concessions booth and have a look at their cash box. Technically I was not in charge of it—it belonged to the grocery store people who'd donated the food—but as the event planner, I could go wherever I chose, or at least so I had decided.

"Yes," Brooke persisted. "And like you do now, you loved animals so much. Especially birds, which is why I wasn't surprised to find you here looking at these guys."

"The birds are handsome," I conceded.

"I can't believe you don't remember going to that petting zoo. You were crazy about it. But I'll bet you do remember the promise we made to each other, don't you? I flat-out won't believe that you've forgotten about *that*."

"About what?"

Brooke's eyes narrowed. For the first time since I had met her, she looked . . . I'd have to call it troubled, and uneasy. "You mean you don't remember? I know, sure it was silly, but we were so serious. We swore! You even insisted that we do a blood pact, where we cut our fingers and mingled the blood together and then spit on it. You're telling me you don't remember what we promised each other?"

I groaned internally. Now what?

"Oh, sure. Yeah, I remember. It was just a dumb kid thing, though. I'd forgotten for the moment."

The expression on her face did not change.

"What? What did we promise?" she asked. Her eyes were intent, watching me.

"Oh, you know," I said, shrugging. "That we'd always be friends. And we are, of course! It was kind of lucky in a way that I fell so hard for—" I fumbled for the name for a moment. "Uh, Ashton. I mean, it brought us back together again after all these years. It's been so great spending this fall with you, Brooke," I continued, pouring on the charm. "I'm glad I got this chance. That's what you meant, isn't it?"

There was a long silence.

"Yes," she said at last. "Yes, that's what I meant."

16

I COULD NOT SPARE ATTENTION FOR BROOKE'S worries about what I did or did not remember regarding some childhood pact she claimed she had shared with her cousin. I was confident that I could win her back with a little attention, some girlish chitchat in our rooms that evening, and some enthusiastic praise for her part in the day's activities. I had seen her in the company of a thin, bespectacled boy earlier in the day, so that might be a fruitful subject of conversation. Perhaps there was a fledgling romance under way? Luckily the boy was not attractive enough to tempt me, so I didn't have to worry about restraining my acquisitive instincts. Brooke was welcome to him.

However, our cozy nighttime chat was not to be.

When we got home, both of us exhausted from the excitements of the day, she was unusually silent and thoughtful, and soon after a late dinner, she retired to her room. When I tapped on the door, there was a long silence, and then Brooke's voice, sounding pretend-groggy.

"Oh, I'm sorry, Morgan, but I was asleep. I'm awfully tired. Can whatever it is wait until morning?"

I looked with raised eyebrows at the line of light showing underneath her door. My cousin Brooke was *not* a practiced deceiver. "Sure," I said. *All the more time for me to count my earnings*, I thought.

I had a long soak in the hot tub and emerged refreshed and relaxed and glowing with well-being. I went to my room and, after locking the door, spread the day's takings over the bed. When I had counted it over several times, I added it to the rest of my stash. I had a total of $5,364 secreted in various pockets of Janelle's otherwise-empty suitcase—a satisfying sum, though hardly enough to set me up for life. But no matter; I was certain I would always be able to raise enough money for my needs, wherever my life might lead me.

I patted the money affectionately and locked it up. I went to the kitchen to make myself a hot drink that would coax me into the deep sleep I craved as the fitting end to a perfect day. On my way back to my bedroom I noticed that Brooke's light was still on. I paused and listened at the door.

I heard the faint slap of something being laid out on the surface of her desk. Could she be playing solitaire, with a pack of real, as opposed to virtual, cards? Oh well. I'd have thought her tablet would have been handier to play on than an actual deck of cards, but that was her lookout. I continued on to my room.

There I sipped my cocoa and stretched luxuriously. I fell asleep with a smile on my face and the sound of remembered applause in my ears.

Brooke was up and dressed by the time I woke, so no opportunity for cousinly confidences then, either.

"Morgan, dear, I hope you won't mind, but Brooke and I thought we'd have a little mother-daughter day today, just the two of us," said Aunt Antonia as I joined them at the breakfast table. "I know you must be exhausted after all your work in the past few weeks, and I'm sure you have lots of homework to do. Your teachers will be expecting you to make up some of the material you've missed because of the benefit." She smiled. "Your uncle Karl will be here if you need anything."

"No he won't," said Uncle Karl, pausing in tapping out a text on his phone. "I've got to go in to the Ravena office. There's a backlog of paperwork that I need to finish up, and we've got a new load of pickups being delivered this afternoon. Count me out for the day."

"Oh," said Aunt Antonia, disconcerted. "Well, perhaps you'd better come with Brooke and me after all, then. I'm sorry—I don't want you to feel left out, or stuck alone at home here."

I waved this off. "No, no," I said, smiling benevolently on them both. "You two go and have a good time together. I guess you don't get much time for the two of you, with me hanging around."

This remark produced a flurry of pleas from both mother and daughter to accompany them.

"Thank you," I said. "But you're right, Aunt Antonia. I have a lot of schoolwork to make up. Honest, I'm better off staying at home."

In the end it took me a good two hours, and several more refusals to join them, to get them out of the house. This was one of Mrs. Barnes's regular days off, so she left too, and the house was empty except for me. I realized that, with the exception of yesterday morning when everybody had been at Hidden Hollow, this had never happened in the two and a half months that I had lived here.

So. That being the case, what should I do next? Never mind homework. Janelle, that home-wrecker, was likely to make her existence known in a week or so, and I would be booted out of here. Let *her* worry about my/ our grades.

I remembered my intention to search Uncle Karl's desk when I had the opportunity. There wasn't going to be a better time than today. Yes, and what *had* Brooke been up to last night? If it'd been a series of games of solitaire, I ought to be able to find a deck of cards in her room. I smiled, anticipating a peaceful day nosing around in other people's business.

Brooke's room first, as this would probably be a quick job. I doubted that I would find much of interest secreted in her underwear drawer, so if I found some playing cards, I would be done.

She did have some modest jewelry—a gold bracelet and a ruby ring—of which I made a mental note. The few other items were costume pieces, pretty enough, but worthless. Her clothes were familiar to me by now: utilitarian T-shirts, sweaters, and jeans. I found a sketchbook with some halfway decent drawings by her and some sick-making poetry, also by her. Books, a few stuffed animals, and a doll from childhood days. Her computer revealed that she had done research on sites relating to homework, horses, and popular music. I uncovered no drugs, dirty magazines, trashy novels, or occult pentacles marked on the floor. Dead boring, in fact. If I had been looking for something with which to blackmail Brooke, I would have been pretty disappointed. There *was* no dark side to Brooke.

There was no deck of cards, either.

What there *was* in the top drawer of her desk was an envelope of photographs. It contained about twenty pictures of two little blond girls. In some photos they held hands, or fed pellets to a goat, or posed next to a miniature donkey. Aha. A petting zoo.

I sat down at the desk and laid the pictures down one by one. Yes, they made the slight slapping noise I had heard the night before. This was what Brooke had been doing; she had been examining photos of herself and her cousin from nine years ago, back when Janelle had come to visit.

You rarely see this format for photos anymore, but a decade ago there were still diehards who took photos with non-digital cameras, hence the envelope of pictures from a facility that processed film.

I looked at them carefully. It took some consideration before I could decide which girl was Brooke and which was Janelle, but eventually I got them sorted out. The problem was that, while I had been a fragile little wisp of a girl at that age, the two cousins were already, at seven years old, big-boned and slightly chubby. They looked almost identical. In a lot of the pictures Janelle was holding a plastic horse—she was horse-mad back then too, I guess.

The images gave no clue as to what the mysterious "pact" might have been, although one did show their clasped hands, each with a thin red cut on the index finger. Brooke had brought the subject up more as a joke than anything else, I thought. It could not have had any real significance, though she didn't like that I didn't recall it.

Why had Brooke been brooding over these last night? The fact that her cousin used to be a bit chunkier than she was today proved nothing. People change.

I shrugged and put the pictures back into the envelope and replaced them in her desk drawer. It couldn't possibly matter, as, sad to say, I was on my way out of here.

I moved on to Uncle Karl and Aunt Antonia's bedroom. Here I found much nicer jewelry, some of which might bring a reasonable amount on eBay or at a pawnshop. The trouble with selling my ill-gotten goods online was that you need a fixed address to ship from, and I might not have one of those for a while. I knew about pawnshops from LA but hadn't seen any here. Mostly they didn't want to do business with a kid like me, so you had to find one with a compliant owner. Still, jewelry was always good—it didn't take up much room, even when you were traveling. And I liked looking at it, especially seeing the gold against my skin, the way it caught the light. I tried on a few pieces and found it rather difficult to take them back off again. I did it, though; I put them back neatly in the jewelry cabinet. No point in getting kicked out before I was ready to go.

I tried on some of Aunt Antonia's clothes, too. These were also a lot better than Brooke's, although pretty conservative. I rooted around in the closet and found a nice little Prada handbag—something she must have used only on occasion, since it was wrapped in tissue paper. This I decided to put into Janelle's suitcase, as Aunt was unlikely to miss it right away. On second thought I went back for a Chanel jacket at the back of the closet, still in plastic from the dry cleaner. It fit me perfectly.

I did a quick tour through Mrs. Barnes's bedroom and was pleasantly surprised to find a sizeable diamond ring in a jewelry box. Nice going, Mrs. Barnes!

The thought of Mrs. Barnes and her ever-ready dusting cloth reminded me. I went back to each of the rooms I had visited and polished every surface I'd touched, along with a lot of other ones, just in case. I didn't want any signs of my presence once I'd gone and they started looking for me.

Now for Uncle Karl's office. Actually, both Aunt and Uncle had home offices, but Aunt's was less used and had fewer papers and files. Obviously she kept most of her work *at* work, while Uncle Karl hauled stuff back and forth and had duplicates in both places. Aunt's office *did* contain papers with some spicy details about a few of her clients, though, so I copied several files and hid them in the suitcase.

I sat down once again at Uncle Karl's desk. Today it

was pristine, without even a mote of dust to mar the walnut finish. I began opening drawers. The usual office supplies on the right, paid bills, user manuals, information about insurance and personal cars, etc., below. On the left were a small drawer and a larger one, likely fitted up for hanging file folders. Both were locked.

Hmm.

Uncle Karl would have the key on his chain. But Uncle Karl was a careful person. What if he lost the key? Undoubtedly he would have another copy somewhere. It would be a small key, I thought, smaller than a door key, more like one for a suitcase. I suddenly recalled the key rack in the mudroom, a piece of board with hooks screwed into it, where random keys were kept.

I went to check. Extra house keys, keys to some of the neighbors' houses (interesting), keys to the lawn tractor and the ATV. There were a few unlabeled small keys, which I tried in the lock. None fit.

I went back to the master bedroom. I hadn't paid much attention to Uncle Karl's closet and bureau earlier, but now I did look, and thoroughly.

I know I can be rather conceited, so I will force myself here to admit that it was pure luck that I found it. I was pulling out a drawer in the bureau when it hit a point where it would come no further. Of course, this might have been due to good carpentry, a stop installed to prevent the drawer from falling out onto the floor. In fact, I was simply annoyed that it was resisting me, and I gave it a vicious yank. It came out, with an accompanying clink as something came loose from its underside.

In the end I had to pull the lower drawers out to their furthest extent and then snake my arm into a thin space in order to grope around underneath to find the item that had fallen, but at last I managed to pinch it between the tips of my middle finger and forefinger.

As I had expected, it was a small key. I sat looking at it, thinking, *My goodness, but that's a lot of trouble to hide a key that protects perfectly innocent business dealings!*

An hour later I was beginning to understand. I am only an unsophisticated fifteen-year-old girl with no knowledge of the Internal Revenue Service or finance or anything technical like that, but it seemed to me that Uncle Karl might be being a little deceitful in his relations with the United States government.

There were several sets of records written in pencil on ledger paper—the kind that is ruled into columns—with cryptic initialed notes at the heads to indicate what each row of figures represented. Let me think: Why would a modern businessman need records on paper locked in his desk, when he had a staff of bookkeepers, each in possession of a computer loaded with the latest financial software?

The advantage of paper is that if one wants to destroy

it, it burns, while digital information is never lost beyond recall. Did I understand exactly what the numbers before me meant? No, I did not. But it was easy to guess that it was something he did not want generally known. After some thought, I took two pages, one that was labeled "SAC," and one "SFA," which I thought might represent this year's sales at his two biggest dealerships. These pages I put into the suitcase with the other things I had taken. Even if he discovered that they were missing, he couldn't start a big hunt for them without having to explain what they were.

Also in the suitcase I placed, with the utmost, loving care, an envelope containing ten thousand dollars. Yes, $10,000. That was what I found in the upper locked drawer, along with a sizeable stash of pain pills. I replaced the envelope of cash with a similar-looking envelope stuffed with play money left over from the benefit horse race, and left the pill bottles alone. Now that I had the key, there was no point in letting him know I had been in his desk. With any luck he would not immediately notice the lack of two sheets of paper and the exchange of play money for real dollars, but if he was in the habit of taking the pills, it was likely he would spot the fact that they had disappeared.

Uncle Karl played poker the last Friday night of every month. I supposed the envelope of cash was meant to fund this activity. Pretty high stakes, but I thought he was a natural gambler, and, I mean, what of it? He could afford it. I'd have to leave here before his next poker night, or else replace it.

Several hours later Uncle returned, satisfied with the new shipment of pickup trucks, and retired to his office. I waited, in my usual state of alert serenity, hoping that he would not notice anything to concern him, but ready to respond if he did. Nothing happened, and at five o'clock Aunt Antonia and Brooke came home, chattering about the movie they had seen, the clothing they had purchased, and the lunch they had consumed. Uncle Karl appeared and took his evening glass of sherry with Aunt Antonia before our informal meal of salad and soup. Mrs. Barnes was still on her day off, so we were roughing it.

"And have you had a productive day today, Morgan?" Aunt Antonia inquired graciously.

"Oh yes, Aunt, thank you, *very* productive," I said as I helped myself to more clam chowder.

17

IF I'D BEEN SMART, I WOULD HAVE CRAMMED all the valuables I could fit into my suitcase and called a cab to take me to the airport while the family been out for the day on Sunday. I *know* that. I just couldn't do it. I wanted to savor the accolades when I went back to school on Monday after my successful charity benefit. I wanted to make sure Helena knew that Brett had come to *my* event instead of hanging out with her on Saturday. I wanted to pick up the cash from the collection boxes around town.

Since I couldn't bring myself to leave on Sunday or Monday, I should have left on Tuesday. By Tuesday I had been praised and petted to my heart's content, thanked Brett for his support right in front of Helena

DON'T YOU TRUST ME?

and her friends, and emptied the boxes down to the last Canadian nickel. Yet I didn't go.

I went to school and home again, ate wonderful meals and luxuriated in the hot tub and snuggled up in my big, soft bed each night. I took to carrying a little microfiber dust rag around in my jeans pocket and polishing places where I had probably left fingerprints, and where that good housekeeper Mrs. Barnes might not have cleaned lately—the back and underside of my chair in the dining room, the door of my bedroom closet, the flush on the toilet in my private bathroom.

Every time the phone rang, I waited to hear that it was Janelle on the other line, or her friends or neighbors, or even her parents. If either Aunt Antonia or Uncle Karl answered, she would probably not identify herself right away, according to my instructions. Yet that didn't help me much—she'd only ask for Brooke. Unless I answered the phone every single time it rang, a phone call from Janelle meant the end of my life in the Styles household.

At last I was forced to make a decision. Friday night was Uncle Karl's poker game. If I hadn't left by then, I would have to switch the envelope of real money in my suitcase with the fake in his desk drawer, or he'd discover the substitution. Still, I didn't want to go yet. What if he won a lot of money at the game? That would make my departure much sweeter. True, he also might lose a lot of money, but I ignored that possibility. Uncle Karl was a winner, not a loser—I was sure of it.

No more stalling; I would leave on Saturday. The whole family, me included, was scheduled to go over to Granny's house for a tea party with the neighbors, and then we were all supposed to go out to dinner together. If I faked sick and stayed home, that would give me most of Saturday to make my getaway.

Friday evening came, and Uncle Karl went off to meet his pals for a night of cards and single malt whiskey.

"Good luck," I said as he emerged from his office thrusting the envelope, gorged with cash, into the inner pocket of his jacket. "I hope you win lots and lots tonight."

He laughed, touched by my obvious sincerity. "With those good wishes, I can't miss, Morgan. Thanks!"

Aunt Antonia didn't wish him luck; she didn't approve of his poker games. Neither did Brooke. He and I, gamblers both, exchanged surreptitious smiles over the heads of the two puritans. He was gambling on cards; I was gambling on him. If I had been related to him, I'd have said we shared some genes in common, what with our risky behavior and the whiff of dishonesty that hovered over his business dealings.

I settled down with a book in a chair right next to the house telephone. I might be a gambler, but there was no sense in not taking basic precautions. The one call that came in was for Aunt Antonia, and the caller was middle-aged and female, wanting to know if she and Uncle Karl were available for a dinner party. Brooke got a call on her cell. After she answered it, she blushed and retired to her room. Probably that boy.

Brooke had not been her usual chatty self with me since the incident at the petting zoo, but instead was withdrawn and silent when it was the two of us alone in a room together. I hoped that her current moodiness was caused by preoccupation about a guy, and not due to unkind suspicions about me.

The new boyfriend had been witness to an encounter at school the other day, which, if he'd told Brooke about it, probably hadn't helped restore her faith in me. A kid named Rebecca Niles was pestering me at my locker as I was preparing to go home.

"My dad wants those canned goods," she said in an unnecessarily loud voice.

"I don't have any," I said. "I've been busy lately, in case you hadn't heard."

"You *promised*," she said in a whiny voice. "And he already *paid* for them."

The boyfriend, who had been breezing past, slowed. He stopped and had a drink at a nearby water fountain, his ears twitching like a rabbit's.

"Sorry," I said, shrugging. "I'll get them to him later."

"He *needs* them," she said. "He's been doing really

well with the high-end items. He wants more caviar and stuff."

"Look, I can't talk about this now," I said. "I'll stop by this weekend at the store and have a chat with him. Bye." I slammed my locker door shut and walked away.

What was that all about, you ask? Well, see, Rebecca Niles—who was a very low-ranking sophomore—her father owned this little convenience store a couple of blocks from the school. It sold soda and candy and lots of boxed and canned foods for people who didn't want to make a run to the supermarket when they ran out of something. So when I got donations of things like hearts of palm, or grilled artichoke hearts in a jar, well . . .

C'mon. I'd think you'd know me by now. You didn't really believe I was going to donate *all* that fancy canned food to the poor, did you? Give me a break. Poor people don't even like caviar.

The boyfriend definitely heard most of the conversation. But pretty soon it wouldn't matter, because I'd be gone and both he and Brooke would be free to think what they liked.

Anyway, at ten o'clock I mentioned to Aunt Antonia that I could feel a little tickle at the back of my throat. Brooke had not emerged from her bedroom since the call on her cell, so it was Aunt and me in the living room.

"Oh dear, I hope you aren't coming down with something," she said. "I suppose it wouldn't be a surprise if you did, after all the work you've been putting in—sort of a reaction to the stress. Let me make you some tea with honey. That usually helps a little."

I sipped my tea and agreed that it had soothed my fictitious sore throat. My plans required that I be alone in the house the next day—true, Mrs. Barnes would be here part of the time, but in this big house it ought to be easy to avoid her while I made my preparations—so I was careful not to be too reassuring about the state of my health.

I retired to my room at ten thirty. At one thirty a noise woke me, and I lay there listening. Evidently Uncle Karl was returning from his game and not making much attempt to be quiet about it. I had to know whether he had won or lost tonight. I got up and switched on the hall lights, descending to the first floor, where Uncle sat in one of the leather club chairs, having a last drink before bed.

"Morgan! Sweetheart!" A big smile spread over his face at the sight of me. He was pretty lit up, I could tell. "My good luck charm! Your kind wishes brought me luck. I won a packet tonight."

I could have kissed him. He'd come through for me! The gamble had been worth the risk.

However, I couldn't show my elation. In a raspy voice I said, "Congratulations, Uncle Karl."

"What's a matter with your voice?" he inquired,

slurring ever so slightly. "What're you doing up, anyway?"

"Sore throat," I said. "I couldn't sleep."

"Poor kid. Well, we can't have that, can we? I think there's some ibuprofen in the kitchen."

He got up and bumbled around the kitchen for a while, then returned with two pills and a glass of luke-warm water.

"Thanks, Uncle Karl."

He sat finishing his drink while I took the medicine and swallowed the water, grimacing at the supposed pain.

"Yeah—I better get that money to the bank," he murmured, more to himself than to me. "Too much to keep in the house. Askin' for trouble."

I regarded him with disapproval. I did not want him taking that money with him when he left in the morning. "The bank is closed on Saturday," I said in a firm tone.

"Oh, right," he said. I rose and took my water glass to the kitchen.

"Good night, Uncle Karl," I said. "Congratulations on your win."

"Well, get some sleep. That ibuprofen must be working. Your voice sounds better already."

Oops. I gave a pathetic little cough and a wan smile, and shuffled off upstairs.

Needless to say, I did not go back to bed. He had

agreed with me that the bank would be closed, but for all I knew there were other branches, perhaps even ones closer to Granny's house, that might be open. I wanted to make the switch tonight, before I lost the chance. I waited the tedious half hour while Uncle Karl puttered around, getting ready for bed. To my relief, I heard him cross the living room and go into his study. Holding my breath and straining my senses, I heard the faint jingle of keys, then the click as he unlocked and opened the desk drawer, then a further click as he shut it.

Attaboy, Uncle Karl.

He came upstairs and went into the master bedroom. I still did not dare to go back down. It would take him time to get into bed and go to sleep. I nearly fell asleep myself, waiting. In fact, I think I kind of did. My watch said 3:00 a.m. the next time I looked.

I got up and went downstairs. I can all but float when I want to, so I didn't make a sound on the stairs. I was in and out of the study in less than a minute, a fat envelope thrust into my underpants, under my nightgown, in case anybody spotted me on the way upstairs. But no, all was still, and I slipped into my bed much, much richer than I had left it. How much richer? I would leave that discovery until the morning light.

"May I have some more coffee, please, Mrs. Barnes? Oh, Karl, I meant to tell you: the Luttrells are leaving today, and they asked us to water their plants," Aunt Antonia said. She pushed a small bag across the table toward me. "Here, Morgan. I found these cough lozenges in our bathroom cabinet. They should help your throat."

Uncle Karl looked up from his cell. We were at breakfast—at least Aunt and Uncle and I were. Brooke was still in her room.

"Oh? For long?" he inquired.

"A week, I think. We don't need to go over there until Wednesday because she watered them last night. There's a funeral in the Midwest they have to go to. Her sister. Only forty-three, but she had some rare cancer. It's been a long, horrible illness."

"Mmm, too bad," said Uncle Karl. He stabbed the yellow of his egg with a fork, and it bled messily over his toast. "Hope I keel over dead when I'm playing poker, as drunk as a lord and holding a royal flush."

"*Really*, Karl!" Aunt glanced at me, and her lips tightened. He wasn't supposed to say things like that in front of the children, I guess.

I smiled benevolently upon this morbid conversation. I was struggling to keep up the pretense that I was in too bad a shape to go with them today. Dear, *dear* Uncle Karl had come through for me. That envelope had contained $18,620 in well-worn bills. The wonderful, clever man had nearly doubled my money!

I swallowed the last of my orange juice and, remembering to cough, made my exit. "If you don't mind," I said, "I think I'll go back to bed. I'm awfully sleepy."

"Yes, do, Morgan," Aunt Antonia said. "We'll clear out of here soon and leave you in peace."

I passed Brooke in the hall and gave her a pitiful wave before retiring to my room. She nodded and blushed, averting her face as she passed. Whether it was because she had a bad case of the hots for that boy, or because she was suspicious of my virtue, I could not be bothered to discover. I was leaving today. I just needed to see them off the premises, and I could pack up and go.

Once in my room I started to—well, not worry exactly, but wonder. What if Uncle decided to take the money to the bank this morning? And what if he looked *in* the envelope? It was pretty good fake money, much more convincing than Monopoly or toy dollars, but still, no bank teller would be taken in by it. I sat for an endless time listening, trying to guess whether or not he paid a visit to the study. My ears were also tuned for the house telephone. It would seem a little weird if I had to rush out and answer it, seeing as how I was supposed to be sick and asleep, but too bad, I'd have to do it if it rang.

At last I heard the sounds of them leaving. Car doors slammed, and they drove off.

I smiled. Janelle hadn't called. Maybe she *was* pregnant, and that was why I hadn't heard from her. Anyway, it was not my problem anymore.

18

WHILE I PACKED, METHODICALLY GOING THROUGH my desk and bureau drawers, sliding clothes off hangers and shoes off shoe trees and polishing away my fingerprints, I brooded upon the unfairness of my expulsion from this suburban Eden. Why should I leave Brooke in the sole possession of this palatial house complete with lavish meals, loving family, and cute little sports cars?

It was Janelle's fault. Well, and perhaps there was a smidgeon of blame to be laid on Brooke, who had so lately become suspicious and grudging in her friendship. Aunt Antonia, too, tended to side with her dearest Brooke. If only we could get rid of troublesome Janelle, two-faced Brooke, and unfair Auntie! How fabulous if this household were to be made up of Uncle Karl, Grandma, and me. Oh, and *dear* Mrs. Barnes too, to cook and clean and deal with the dirty laundry I dropped on the floor.

Speaking of Mrs. Barnes, she popped her head around my door at noon. I had kept the bed unmade, so I was able to slip back into it, fully clothed, the blankets pulled up around my neck, when I heard her footsteps on the stairs. Seeing I was awake, she advanced into the room with a lunch tray. Gazing down at it (a small vase with one late rose for decoration, chicken salad with sugar snap peas and slivered almonds, an herbed goat cheese with crackers, and a small wedge of cherry pie for dessert), I could not help but feel that she was deliberately tormenting me with the excellence of her cooking and homemaking skills. She announced that she was off to do the grocery shopping. I nodded—I had known she would be, and was counting on her absence so I could finish my preparations and leave.

"Thank you, Mrs. Barnes," I said mournfully. She was the one I would miss the most, by far. I reminded myself to step into her room for that great big diamond ring before I left. Oh, Mrs. Barnes, a source of good things right to the very end.

I waited until I'd heard her car pull out of the driveway, and got back to work. I tucked Brooke's little collection of jewelry into Janelle's suitcase and then added

Aunt Antonia's. To my surprise and delight I found a Rolex in Uncle Karl's sock drawer. Where had that come from? It hadn't been there the other day. He must have won that as well as cash in the poker game. I'd also found a money belt in his drawer, so I split up the cash; ten thousand in hundreds, the least bulky denomination, was concealed in the belt under my shirt, and the rest went back into the suitcase. I didn't like the idea of putting all my golden eggs in one basket.

I had just, with considerable difficulty, zipped the bulging case shut and hauled it downstairs, when the phone rang.

There was no rational reason to answer it. I was leaving—nothing could stop me now. But I did. I suppose it was because I'd trained myself to lunge for the phone the previous week, waiting for Janelle to call. And guess who it was.

"Oh, good, Brooke. It's me, Janelle. Look, you've got to come and pick me up at the bus station. I haven't got any more money, and this place is creepy."

"Ah, Janelle," I said, my voice flat. "You're here? Here at the Albany bus depot, you mean?"

"Well, of course," she said crossly. "Where else?"

Um, how about the San Jacinto Mountains, spending my hard-earned money on junk food and pregnancy tests? That was where she was supposed to be.

"I got *bored*," she said, like I should have known,

which I suppose I should have. "Nobody's answering the phone at home, and the voicemail is full, so I can't even yell at them anymore. I called one of my friends, and she thought I was crazy. She said my parents went to *Brazil*, and they're staying there for *months*. So I bought a ticket east with the rest of the money because I didn't know what else to do. You've just got to talk your mom and dad into letting me stay. Oh! And I'm not pregnant. Isn't that great? Such a relief. It took me *days* to get here, and I'm so sick of being on a stupid bus. I'm, like, filthy dirty, and I stink because I haven't had a shower in ages. So come and get me."

"You make it sound so appealing," I said absently. Whiny *and* smelly, what a combination! But I was thinking. If I hung up the phone, I could head straight for the airport and forget about her. The problem was, the family and Mrs. Barnes would be back before too long. If Janelle behaved true to form, she would keep calling and calling until she reached somebody here after I hung up. Yeah, it would take a while for them to sort out what had happened, but the next thing they'd do is call the police, and the police would alert the airport, the train station, and the bus terminal, and everybody would start looking for a blond girl traveling with Janelle's ID, who had paid cash.

Not good.

I'd tossed my own ID back in LA, not realizing how

it might come in handy someday. If only I'd had more time, I could've faked some up, using the papers I'd liberated from the school filing system or Aunt Antonia's desk. But there was no time! Pain-in-the-butt Janelle was, as usual, causing all kinds of complications.

One thing was for sure: I needed to get myself and my overstuffed suitcase out of here before anybody came back home. My eye fell upon the rack of keys in the mudroom. There was a new set of keys, labeled with the Luttrells' address, hanging on it. I grabbed it and returned to the living room, peering out the front windows. Yes, I could see the house.

"Bro-o-o-ke!" Janelle's voice did this irritating slide up and down the musical scale. "When are you co-o-om-ing?"

"Right away," I said.

When the Styles family had left to go to Grandma's, they'd taken two cars. The senior Styleses took the Cadillac, but Brooke took her Miata because she planned to continue on to somewhere else afterward. She'd been holding these whispered phone conversations on her cell lately, so I supposed it was a rendezvous with her new boyfriend she had in mind.

That left a choice between the Jeep and Uncle Karl's cherished Corvette, yet *another* sexy little roadster this family owned and wouldn't let me drive. *He* hogged it all the time, and it was even an automatic, so I wouldn't have any trouble with it. I snagged the 'Vette keys off the Peg-Board. Well, I mean, wouldn't you?

I put the top down, tossed my suitcase into the trunk, and backed out of the garage. I paused in the driveway for a moment, put the parking brake on, and ran back into the house, and returned a moment later after one last wipe for fingerprints, with a bright scarf and a big pair of sunglasses, both belonging to Aunt Antonia. They might provide at least a little disguise.

Yowza! Great car! I roared around the corner of Woodcrest and Grapevine doing fifty-five, the passenger-side wheels riding up over the neighbors' front lawn a little. If it weren't that the car was so conspicuous, I'd have been tempted to keep going, maybe driving south for the winter. But no, they'd catch me for sure, so I eventually slowed and drove sedately along Central Avenue toward downtown Albany, stopping at every red light.

It occurred to me that I had no idea where the bus terminal was. Oh well. Probably near the government buildings. I finally had to ask somebody. It was tucked away from sight on a side street like they were ashamed of it, which maybe they were, because Janelle was right about it being creepy.

Janelle was standing out front looking pissed off, with this cheap little nylon bag at her feet that held all her worldly goods.

When I pulled up in front of her in the red Corvette, she smiled and waved. When I got out, though, and she focused on my face, half hidden though it was by scarf and shades, she frowned.

"It's me. Brooke," I said, grabbing her bag. "You're Janelle, right?"

"Yes, but . . ."

"You don't remember me, do you? It's been so long since we've seen each other. Way back when we were seven years old." I tossed her bag into the trunk next to mine and slammed the trunk shut, superfast so she wouldn't notice that my bag was really *her* bag. "Hop in."

She hesitated for a second, but then climbed into the passenger seat.

"Sorry," she said. "You remind me of somebody, but I guess . . ." Her voice trailed off.

"I remind you of *you*," I said, pulling the scarf tighter around my throat. "We look a lot alike. No wonder! We're cousins."

"I guess," she said, looking doubtful.

Well, poop. I'd been counting on her memory of me being hazy. Still, I recognized *her*, so I suppose it made sense she'd recognize me. I just had always figured her for a dim bulb.

However, I only had to keep her fooled for another twenty minutes or so. The thing to do was to distract her.

"D'you like to drive really fast?" I asked.

"Like, *how* fast? This is a supercool car," she added, finally noticing the red streak of gorgeousness she was sitting in.

"How fast? Let me show you," I said, and put my foot on the accelerator.

"*Slow down, Brooke!* Watch out for that *truck!*"

"Isn't this fun?" I inquired, slowing down as we pulled into the Styleses' neighborhood.

"Holy— Do Aunt Antonia and Uncle Karl know how fast you drive?" Janelle was panting and holding on to her bucket seat, her eyes wild. Weirdly, I found that I resented Janelle calling them "Aunt" and "Uncle." By now I felt that they were *my* aunt and uncle.

"No," I said, "they think I'm a totally safe driver. Which I am, of course. I just like to let it all out sometimes. It's good for the engine—it cleans the carbon out of the piston valves, or something." Uncle Karl had said that to me once, and I'd noted the explanation down for the future.

"I doubt there's even one flake of carbon left in this car's engine, in that case," Janelle said. "Are you *sure* that cop wasn't signaling to you? Because it looked to me like he was."

"That cop already had somebody pulled over. He was much too busy to bother with me," I replied, swooping up the driveway to the Luttrells' house, which was around the corner from the Styleses' place. "Here we are."

Janelle looked around. "That's funny," she said. "Somehow I remember your house kind of differently. Wasn't there a little garden over there? Remember, we had a dolls' tea party there. And wasn't the front door over on the other side? And wasn't the garage in the back?"

"We had it remodeled," I said, jumping out and opening the trunk for Janelle's stuff.

"Yeah? You changed the position of the door? How come?"

I rolled my eyes. Who knows why suburban homeowners do anything? Who cares? "Actually, you're remembering it wrong. We did have it remodeled, but the door and the garage are where they always were." I pulled the bunch of keys out of my jeans pocket and, taking a wild guess, stabbed at the lock with one of them.

Oops. Wrong one. I tried another.

Janelle looked at my hands, busy with the keys. The tag saying "Luttrell" on it slid into view as, finally, the key turned in the lock. I grabbed the whole bunch, covering the tag with my hand, and pushed the door open.

"Welcome to our home," I said, gripping her by the elbow and maneuvering her inside.

The Luttrells evidently really, really liked fake flowers. The place looked like a funeral home all ready for a viewing, minus the corpse. There were massive arrangements of lilies and orchids in chest-high vases stationed around here and there, and smaller bouquets of silk roses and baby's breath dotted the occasional tables. The fireplace was filled with fake autumn leaves and New England asters, and the mantelpiece and chandeliers dripped with woven chains of curly chrysanthemums and red plastic berries. I expected to hear a blast of organ music and see some guy in black sidle out in front of the hearth and intone, "My friends, we are gathered here today to pay tribute—"

"Wow," said Janelle, looking around herself.

"Yeah," I agreed. "That's my mom: flower-mad. Only, she doesn't have a green thumb, so . . ." I waved vaguely at the massed greenery. Since Aunt Antonia was supposed to come over and water the plants on Wednesday, *some* of them must have been real, but the place smelled of Scotchgard and lemon furniture polish and not at all of dirt or growing things. I walked forward cautiously, feeling like I needed a machete to hack through the jungle. I was trying to figure out the layout of the house so I wouldn't show Janelle into a broom closet or something.

Here was the dining room. More banks of fake flowers, gladioli this time, standing sentinel around the room, and a huge arrangement on the table of severed sunflower heads surrounding a faux pumpkin. Next was the kitchen, with hanging baskets of ivy and plastic gourds everywhere. Ah. *That* door—the one with the lock on it— probably led to the cellar. Unlike lots of LA houses, these northeastern homes usually have a cellar.

I turned to Janelle, who had followed me, and plastered a huge smile across my face.

"I hope you don't mind, but I think the best place for you to stay is in the guest bedroom off the rec room downstairs in the basement. You'll see, it's perfectly nice, but kind of underground. It's only that my mother's sister and her family are coming to stay, and they'll fill up the bedrooms upstairs."

"Really? I thought your mother was an only child."

Honestly. Janelle was *so* annoying. "Oh, did I say sister? I meant sister-in-law. Would you like a soda, or would you rather go right downstairs and take a shower?"

"A soda would be nice, but"—her forehead knotted up with thought— "the only sister-in-law she'd have if she's an only child would be *my* mother, and she's in Brazil."

"That's right," I said, nodding enthusiastically as I rooted around in the refrigerator. Oh good, a ginger ale. I inserted it into her fist and yanked open the door, revealing a set of descending stairs. Yes!

"She *is* in Brazil, but"—I flipped the light switch on to illuminate the steps—"she's coming home. Now, why don't you run downstairs and freshen up before everybody gets here?" I gave her a gentle push through the doorway onto the first stair. She stopped there, turning to look at me. Her shoulder and arm were still inside the kitchen, even though the rest of her was in the basement.

"You're joking! My parents are coming here?"

"Of course!" Couldn't she just *move*, for crying out loud? Was I going to have to shove her down the stairs?

"Why didn't you tell me before?"

"It was a surprise, silly!" I said. "Now go on and be sure and lather up good, because frankly, Cousin, you're a teeny bit fragrant, if you know what I mean."

"Wow, that's amazing! I can't believe it!"

"Believe it, Janelle," I said between gritted teeth.

"Okay, then, give me my bag so I have something to change into."

I thought about this. Who knew what she had in that bag? Her phone, probably, with which she could call the police.

"I'll bring it down when I come. You go ahead. I want to organize some snacks."

"Fine. Which way is the bathroom?"

"Straight through the main room and then hang a left," I said.

"Okay. But, Brooke?"

"Yes?"

"Can you bring, like, some fruit or something? I feel like I've been eating Cheetos for years."

"I would be delighted. Fresh fruit compote coming right up."

"Good. See you in a few minutes." She turned and began to descend the steps.

Finally.

I eased the door shut and turned the lock. As I walked away, a tiny little voice floated up to me from below.

"Brooke? Hey, Brooke? You can't take a left, 'cause it ends in a cement wall. Don't you even know the rooms in your own house? Brooke? Brooke, this is a *work*shop. I don't see a bathroom, or a bedroom either. Brooke?"

I smiled. Tiresome Janelle had been disposed of for a few days, anyway.

19

I WAS HUMMING A TUNE AS I LOOKED AROUND
to make sure I wasn't leaving any incriminating evi-
dence behind me. I still had the little blue dust cloth in
my pocket, so I went through wiping my prints. No
doubt I'd left *some* at the Styleses' house, but not many.
Darling Mrs. Barnes was so good at dusting and polishing, and I had done a pretty good job myself. Since
my fingerprints weren't on file and there were lots of
people in and out of that house besides family members, it was unlikely they'd have any reason to fix on a
stray pair of prints in a public room. I'd been meticu-
lous in my own bedroom and bath.

Anyway, it wasn't like I was going to be wanted in
a homicide or anything. Aunt Antonia would be at

the Luttrells' to water the plants in a day or two. And I *had* left Janelle with a ginger ale. If she rationed it, she'd be fine. Even if she didn't, there was probably a source of water down there somewhere. Isn't that, like, where the pipes for the water come into the house in the first place?

The only thing that would happen to her would be that she'd lose a pound or two from fasting, and *that* wouldn't hurt her. She'd come out of this whole experience a sadder but wiser young woman, *and* with a trimmer waistline. Probably.

"Brooke? Brooke, open this door!" The basement door rattled as Janelle banged on it.

I rolled my eyes. I was beginning to feel a bit put-upon—all that yelling was giving me a headache.

I am a thief. It is my nature, and I am comfortable with it. What I am not is a kidnapper, or whatever I had become by shutting her up in the basement. Okay, the actual maneuvering of Janelle into the basement didn't cause me a single twinge of guilt, but now I was beginning to think. Wasn't kidnapping a federal crime? Like, with the FBI hot on your trail?

I started to feel more and more irritated. It was entirely her fault that she was in this situation, and if you thought about it, the whole thing was super-unfair to *me*. If anything happened to that idiot, they would come after me like I was Genghis Khan or something, when all I asked was to be left alone. For one moment I debated letting her out and pretending it was a joke.

No, I couldn't do that. She'd tip them off and they'd catch me, whether I fled by bus, train, or plane. What I needed was to make sure she didn't die or injure herself seriously while she was shut up in here, because either one was bound to cause trouble for me down the line.

Ah. Her cell phone. That was it. I dumped out the contents of her bag, mentally reviewing everything I remembered about her means of communication. Her parents had taken her original phone away so she couldn't talk to Ashton Whoever. Then she'd bought a disposable, but it had run out of juice because there was no electricity at the cabin.

I found it and turned it on.

Surprise! There *was* a charge on it, 100 percent full. Oh, well maybe you could charge it while you were riding on the bus or something and that's why it was working. Since it was a cheap disposable, I was almost certain the authorities wouldn't be able to trace it once I'd dumped it in a trash can.

I pocketed it, figuring that after I landed somewhere, I'd give the Styleses a call and warn them about the Luttrells' unexpected guest. As a bonus, I'd also get a chance to say a fond farewell to Brooke and my happy life on the outskirts of Albany.

"Don't worry," I said, lifting my voice to be heard over

the banging on the door. "Somebody will be here to let you out tomorrow morning. Now, don't gulp that soda down all at once. You'll want it later."

I tossed the bag into a corner, took the keys labeled "Luttrell," and headed for the door. After locking up, I would tuck the keys under the doormat on the front porch so there would be no delay in opening the house up tomorrow when they went to rescue Janelle.

See? I can be thoughtful when I try. But will I get any credit for it? Not likely.

I opened the front door.

"Morgan! What are you doing here? What's Daddy's car doing in the driveway?"

I reared back as though I'd discovered a rattlesnake on the doormat.

Worse than a rattlesnake, it was Brooke.

After a *lo-o-ng* millisecond, during which my brain processed this information, I said, "Oh, Brooke, good! I'm so glad you're here!"

Lying comes as naturally to me as breathing. When I'm stumped for what to say, I automatically blurt out the exact reverse of what I actually feel. I pulled her inside, taking care to flip the lock on the door as I closed it. I had no idea what I was going to do next, but it only made sense to hinder her if she got any ideas about making a sudden exit, screaming.

"Morgan, what's going on? Hey!" Her eyes narrowed

and her voice deepened with suspicion. "Isn't that my mom's Hermès scarf you're wearing?"

I ignored the last question, while filing the information away in my mind. (Hermès, eh? Might be worth some bucks.) I made my eyes go big and wide. I shushed her, my finger at my lips.

"There's something in the basement," I whispered.

"What?" she whispered back.

At that moment Janelle, bless her little heart, chose to let out an infuriated scream and hammer on the basement door. It was several rooms away from the front hall, where Brooke and I stood, but clearly audible.

Brooke jumped and brought one hand to her mouth.

"Who is it?" she breathed.

"I don't know. I came over here to water the plants and . . . and . . ." My brain scrabbled frantically for some reason why I would come over here when I was supposedly down sick with a vicious cold. "And feed the cat," I concluded triumphantly.

"What cat?" Brooke was looking skeptical. She crossed her arms across her chest. What was wrong with the girl? Whatever had happened to sweet, trusting Brooke? She continued, "The Luttrells don't have a cat. Mrs. Luttrell says dogs and cats just—you know, pee all over everything. She's really house-proud, and I've heard her say she couldn't understand why anybody would keep an animal in their home."

"It's not theirs," I explained, still in an urgent murmur. "That's why she forgot it was there when they left in such a hurry. It's their niece's. She begged them to take care of it while she was in the hospital for an operation. Like you said, Mrs. L hates cats 'cause they pee all over everything, so she said she'd only keep it in the basement. Then she heard about her sister dying—not the niece's mother, a different one—and she rushed off without remembering about the cat in the basement. So she called your mother to ask her to take care of the cat, but nobody was home except for me. I came over here, even though I'm sick"—I coughed illustratively—"to feed the poor kitty, and I heard somebody screaming and swearing and kind of *growling* in the cellar. It was *awful*!"

Brooke opened her mouth to question me further—perhaps to inquire why I found it necessary to drive the five hundred feet between the two houses in her father's red Corvette—but apparently I had raised my voice on the last few words of my explanation, and that'd attracted the attention of the beast in the basement. Janelle was using something or other to bang on the underside of the floor where we stood. Maybe a broom handle?

"I can hear you whispering up there, you horrible person! Is that you, Brooke Styles?" Janelle said, in a menacing voice that penetrated the floorboards. "'Cause if it is, I'm going to *kill* you!"

Brooke's mouth dropped open. She turned to stare at me, wide-eyed.

"We'd better call the police," she said, so faintly that I had to strain to hear her.

I couldn't have her doing *that*. I looked around and saw a pad of paper and pencil on a table near the door. I darted over to it and wrote: *Wait. Really, really worried about poor cat.* I underlined the last "really" and held the note out to her.

She nodded slowly as she read. She took the pad from me and wrote: *Yes, but police will find it.*

Let me try something, I wrote back. *Stay here & tap foot.* I demonstrated by tapping my foot—two short, sharp taps.

"What are you doing?" snarled Janelle from below. "I can hear you, you know."

Brooke looked at me questioningly. I wrote: *She's underneath us, away frm bsmnt dr. I'll sneak over.* I pointed toward the kitchen. *& U keep her here. I'll open door & call cat. Then call cops. Please? Don't want cat 2 get shot.*

Brooke looked horrified at the idea of the innocent kitty—already abandoned and starving—winding up as collateral damage in a SWAT team intervention. She hesitated, torn between a natural desire to get out of the house and the possibility of rescuing an animal in need, and then nodded. She gave two more taps with her heel on the floor. I flashed a thumbs-up sign and started toward the kitchen.

She and I were in each other's line of sight all the way until I entered the kitchen. The cellar door was around the corner. I looked back at her and nodded again before disappearing into the far room. By way of variety, Brooke rapped repeatedly on the wall this time.

"Stop that!" snapped Janelle. "You're driving me crazy." To my relief, her voice sounded small and far away from me—coming from below Brooke, in fact.

I opened the basement door without making a sound, but did not trouble myself with calling a nonexistent cat. I waited for one long beat and then stepped back into the dining room, staring at Brooke, my face slack with horror. I said nothing but pointed helplessly back into the kitchen.

After pausing only to give a few more distracting thumps on the wall, Brooke approached on tiptoe, her face one big question mark.

What? she mouthed at me.

Just trust me, I mouthed back. *Go look.* I pointed down the stairs. She crept closer to the basement door, as though to the edge of a flaming abyss.

She peered into the gloom, and then looked back at me. *"What?"* she whispered.

I gestured for her to step forward, one tiny little step down. *Come on, Brooke, don't you trust me?*

She made a face, reluctant to place herself in greater proximity to the terror below but unable to overcome her better instincts about the welfare of the cat.

She stepped forward onto the first step.

This time I didn't have the luxury of letting her go all the way down the stairs under her own steam. I gave her a good push. Unbalanced, she fell, grabbing at the railing as she slid down the steps. I slammed the door on her and turned the lock.

A few loud bumps, a shriek of terror, and then a groan relieved any apprehensions I might have felt about my former cousin. A thud followed by silence would have been far more ominous. Obviously she had slowed her fall by clutching the handrail. I'd guess that she would have nothing more to show for being pushed down a flight of stairs than a bruise or two.

Hardly any need to get the cops involved at all, *I* would think.

I could hear Janelle galumphing through the basement, ready to repel this intruder. "What are you doing? What happened?" she shouted. Then, after a moment observing the new resident of the cellar, "Who are *you*?"

"Don't hit me!" Brooke shouted.

"Well, I will if you don't tell me who you are!" Evidently Janelle was still brandishing the broomstick or whatever.

"I'm—I'm—" Just in time Brooke remembered the threat to kill her issued through the floorboards. Even then she couldn't bring herself to lie outright. "I'm a neighbor. What have you done to the cat?"

"What cat?"

I decided to interrupt.

"Girls, it is time for me to leave you," I said in a loud voice. "I am sorry to go away and desert you in such an uncomfortable situation, but I am afraid you have left me no choice. I mean, honestly," I added, unable to resist expressing my sense of grievance, "this is all on you, not me. In the future try to keep your noses out of other people's business, will you? It's *your* best interests I'm thinking of here."

There was a silence below; perhaps they were mulling over my advice.

"Who *is* that?" demanded Janelle. "Do you know her? Is that really Brooke Styles, my cousin?"

"Brooke? No! I'm—that is to say—"

"Well, pardon me for interrupting," I said, feeling a bit put out that they were chatting with each other instead of attending to me at this, my moment of triumph, "but I wanted to reassure you that I will make sure somebody comes to get you out tomorrow morning, so there is no reason to panic. Share that ginger ale"—in my mind the ginger ale had expanded to a case of sodas and several twelve-slice pizza pies—"so you don't become dehydrated, and you will be fine. Brooke, I must thank you and your family for your hospitality. I would have to say that it has been"—I found myself waxing positively sentimental here—"the best few months of my life so far, living with you."

Silence. Then: "So . . . she's *not* Brooke? You mean, *you're* Brooke Styles?" I heard Janelle ask.

"Well . . . are you by any chance Janelle?" Brooke said.

"Of course I am."

"Then in that case, yeah, I am Brooke Styles," Brooke admitted.

"Then—who is *she*?"

"I have *no* freaking idea," said Brooke.

My high opinion of Brooke was beginning to take some hits. All that shiny innocence seemed like it was wearing off. I mean, "freaking" sounded awfully close to swearing to me. However, that was none of my concern, and I supposed I should have expected her to be a bit taken aback by this turn of events. The main point was that I was making a serious effort to behave in a gracious and courteous manner toward this representative of my host family here in Albany, and she was paying no attention to me whatsoever.

"Well, I'm sorry to interrupt your conference," I said, "but I did want to say good-bye, and thank you for your kindness. Oh," I added, "and especially, please tell Mrs. Barnes thank you. She was wonderful."

"Who is Mrs. Barnes?" asked Janelle, sounding bewildered.

"Our housekeeper," explained Brooke.

"Fine. I don't get it, but come on," said Janelle, and I heard noises indicating that they were climbing up the stairs. Evidently the two of them had decided that they were on the same team, and were coming to plead with me. I took a moment to polish the doorknob and woodwork. A sudden assault, as if from all four of their fists, made the door tremble under my hand. I treated this commotion with the scorn it deserved. Not *exactly* the sort of behavior that would induce me to let them out.

"Hey, you! Whoever—*whatever* you are out there—I suppose you *are* that girl I met at the LA airport? That's you, isn't it?"

I could see no reason to deny it. The self-involved little twerp had never asked for my name.

"Yes, that's me," I agreed. "Once I got here and looked around, I realized I'd have to be crazy to leave. You girls have no idea how good you've got it. Most people would be happy to saw off their right arm if it meant they could trade their lives for yours."

She ignored my last remark. "So you're going to go off and leave us here?"

"That's right," I said. I studied my surroundings with an analytical eye. The whole episode with Brooke hadn't lasted long enough for me to have left many new fingerprints. Oh! There was Brooke's purse, sitting on the dining room table. Using the dust cloth to shield my fingertips, I picked it up, carried it back to the kitchen, and pawed through it.

Phew! There was her cell phone. It hadn't even occurred to me that she might have had it in the pocket of her jeans. Nice phone, but it was sure to have a tracking device in it, so I had to leave it. I pocketed the twenty dollars and change that was in the wallet.

What else? Maybe I should do something about the pad of paper.

"Don't you think that's kind of harsh?" demanded Janelle's muffled voice.

"Mm-hmm," I agreed. I tore off the sheet of paper we'd used, crumpled it up, and shoved it into my pocket.

Her control broke as she heard me walking away toward the front hall.

"*Yes!* Yes it *is* harsh! It is really, really cold. You are a very *cold* person."

I halted in my tracks. I laughed aloud, delighted.

"You're right," I said. "You got it—that's what I am, very *cold*. Well, ta-ta, ladies. It's been nice knowing you both."

20

THE CORVETTE AWAITED ME IN THE DRIVEWAY,
glowing like a big candy apple in the autumn sunshine.
I paused for a few seconds with my hand on the hood
and breathed in, enjoying the moment. I was leaving
Albany much richer than when I had arrived, and with
a number of new skills.

It was strange. . . . Coming from cosmopolitan
LA to backwater Albany, you'd have expected I'd find
fewer opportunities and smaller horizons, but actually
it was just the reverse. There were too many people
clawing at too few resources in LA, I decided. From
now on it would be second-tier cities for me—those
that were big enough to contain real wealth but small
enough that many of the inhabitants suffered from a

vague, nagging sense of inferiority. *Those* were the sort of communities that were ripe for my particular set of talents.

And one could keep a horse for a less than exorbitant sum on the outskirts of a smaller city too, and perhaps jump in competitions, or hunt foxes—or coyotes, if no foxes were available. I smiled, contemplating my future as a sort of goddess of the hunt.

I climbed into the car and started the engine, and, waving a jaunty farewell to the neighborhood that had witnessed my greatest successes, I took my departure.

As I was turning onto the main road, Mrs. Barnes's blue VW Beetle, laden with the raw ingredients for another series of her memorable meals, chugged past. Talk about perfect timing! She'd be wondering soon what had happened to me, assuming she looked in on me after putting the groceries away. I felt so good that I was tempted to toot my horn in salute as I sailed by her, but refrained.

I was exhibiting definite signs of maturity.

It was only a twenty-minute trip to the airport—far too short to appreciate driving that lovely car for the last time—and when I had parked the beautiful creature in the short-term lot and extricated myself from the low-slung seat, I heaved a great sigh of regret. Someday I would own a car like that myself. I popped open the trunk and—

Stared aghast into emptiness. There was nothing there, not one diamond ring, not one Chanel jacket or so much as a heap of small change. Nothing. Nada. Zilch.

Everything I had worked so hard for was gone.

I stood stone-still, staring at the nothingness in the trunk of the Corvette.

Brooke. That was the only possible answer. She had seen Daddy's car parked in the neighbors' driveway. Investigating, she'd verified, maybe by looking in the glove compartment, that it in fact was her father's car. Then she had looked in the trunk and seen my—that is, Janelle's—suitcase. Maybe the nosey thing had had the nerve to *open* the suitcase, and had seen . . . what? Mommy's Prada handbag? The contents of Mommy's jewelry box? No doubt. She had sure picked up fast on the fact that I was wearing her mother's scarf.

I growled, low in my throat. That suspicious little beast. *What had she done with my suitcase?*

Had she stashed it behind a bush and then immediately raced to the door in order to confront me as I tried to make my exit? Or had she taken the time to carry it back home? Did I dare to go back to try to retrieve it?

I closed my eyes, trying to see again the scene outside the Luttrells' house. I frowned. What was wrong with this picture?

Where was Brooke's Miata? It wasn't at the Luttrells', and I hadn't seen it in the driveway at the Styleses' place.

Presumably she had spotted the Corvette at the Luttrells' as she'd driven past, so would she have gone to the trouble of putting the Miata away in the garage before chasing me down?

What was Brooke up to, anyway? She had come back early, earlier than her parents. My assumption that she had driven her car so she could go to meet the boyfriend had been proved wrong. So why had she? So she could come back home alone first? Why?

A nasty suspicion tugged at the edges of my mind. Considering her recent behavior, I wondered if it was possible that she had returned early because she wanted to see what I would do when the family members were gone. What if she had parked the Miata a block away and walked back, sneaking around, looking in through the windows and hoping to catch me doing something naughty?

The little snoop. How dare she?

However, I reflected with some satisfaction, she would have plenty of time to meditate on her foolish behavior, trapped in the basement with that nitwit Janelle for twenty-four hours. Maybe I shouldn't be in such a hurry to call and have somebody release them, come to think of it.

If only I knew what she'd done with that suitcase! I ran my tongue over dry lips, calculating.

There *were* some low bushes near the driveway, I

remembered. But were they tall enough to conceal a good-size suitcase?

It wasn't like I had already purchased a ticket and needed to be on time to make the flight. I got back into the car and pulled out of the parking space. Luckily, I hadn't been here long enough to incur the two-dollar fee. In my present mood I'd have rammed the barrier rather than fork over the money, and that would not have been wise.

With my face set in an unaccustomed scowl, I turned the Corvette's nose toward the Styleses' house and romped down on the accelerator.

No suitcase lurked under the juniper bushes next to the driveway. I aimed a vicious kick at one of them and got a long, painful scratch on my ankle for my trouble. I was about to prowl around the rest of the house, poking into every shrub, when I stopped to prod at an uncomfortable and unsightly bulge that had shifted to one side of my waist. I resettled the money belt on my stomach and then—

The money belt. Can you believe I'd forgotten all about it?

The bulge was so fat because the belt was stuffed full with a hundred hundreds. There was ten thousand dollars of poker money in that belt. Okay, it didn't compare with the riches in the suitcase, but it wasn't nothing, either. It would get me far away from here, and I'd have some cash to spend while I was figuring out my next move. I had a few hundred dollars in my wallet, too. I was hardly destitute.

I hesitated, irresolute. I felt suddenly uneasy, remembering how noticeable that Corvette was. I'd heard some background noise when I'd driven up, but had been so focused on finding the suitcase that I hadn't paid any attention, figuring it was neighborhood kids, or maybe Janelle and Brooke banging around in the basement.

I should go, I decided. I took one last look around, scanning for a flash of pink suitcase protruding from the landscape somewhere.

"Hey! Is that you, Morgan Johanssen? Wait a sec, I want to talk to you!"

Now what? A guy on a mountain bike was coming at me, his legs pumping furiously and his face red with fury and exertion. I knew him—it was what's-his-name, a student from SUNY Albany. What was *his* problem? I struggled to recall the details of our little arrangement and failed. Oh, who cared?

"I want my money back!"

"Get in line, Einstein," I said. Hey, that rhymed! I ran to the car and vaulted inside without bothering to open the door. It was clearly time to get out of here. The key was already in the ignition; the Corvette and I roared away, leaving him in the dust.

Oh, right. I guess I forgot to tell you about that whole thing with the frat guys at SUNY Albany. Never mind. It really wasn't important.

Once out on Central Avenue, I drove at the legal speed limit, merging with care and stopping at traffic lights. When a little blue car several vehicles behind me ran a red light, causing oncoming cars to screech to a halt and honk their horns in outrage, I lifted a critical eyebrow.

Some people just shouldn't be allowed to have a driver's license.

I studied the departure boards for a few minutes, trying to decide my destination. I didn't want to draw any more attention to myself than I already would, traveling without a prior reservation and without luggage.

Although the weather was warm for late October in upstate New York, I had been driving around in a convertible with the top down. I shivered a little and began thinking about cities in sunnier climes. Miami? No, too big. I wanted something more provincial. Maybe Richmond, Virginia? That flight was leaving in an hour. And didn't they go fox hunting a lot in Virginia? Sounded okay to me. I moved over to the ticket counter.

"No luggage?" the ticket agent demanded in disapproving tones.

I gave a bored and bratty sigh. "Of course I haven't

got any *luggage*," I said, acting like that was the stupidest question I'd ever heard. "Haven't you ever seen a child of divorce before? I'm like a Ping-Pong ball. I spend a few weeks at *Mom's*, then a few weeks at *Dad's*. I've got a complete wardrobe on both ends. *Duh*."

"No need to be rude," said the agent, staring down her long nose at me. "Your flight departs from gate twelve C. Next?"

This time I didn't fool around. I went and got in line to go through security, submitting to the multiple indignities demanded by airplane travel. This included removing my money belt in *full* view of everyone, thank you *very* much, TSA. I had to run the belt through the X-ray along with my shoes and jacket, and then slip it back under my shirt with twenty pairs of eyes on me the whole while. Finally I moved toward the gate. Lacking a phone with which to occupy myself, like a normal person, I stopped at a newsstand and bought a magazine.

I found a seat in the waiting area around the gate. This wasn't as crowded as it had been in LA, but most of the seats were taken. Almost as soon as I settled down, a small child in a long poufy pink gown with a tiara on her head drifted over and stood staring at me. I ignored her and concentrated on my magazine. It turned out to be about celebrities, something that interested me not at all. Brad and Angelina had adopted another baby, the magazine reported breathlessly. Who were Brad and Angelina?

"What's your name?" the child demanded at last. If this Brad and Angelina couple was so crazy about adopting kids, why couldn't they have adopted this one?

"Cruella De Vil," I said, harking back to a movie I'd seen as a kid. She was this lady who liked to kill and skin black-and-white spotted puppy dogs, so she could make coats out of them. A woman after my own heart.

The evil infant thought about this. "No it's not," she said.

I looked around for the person who was supposed to be in charge of the child. There was a harried-looking woman three seats away, simultaneously feeding a bottle to a baby, rocking it, and hanging on to a barely ambulatory little boy who was struggling to break free from his mother's grasp. She paid no attention to either the little girl or to my annoyed stare. The baby suddenly relinquished its death-hold on the nipple of the bottle and shrieked, like an enraged teakettle. I winced.

"What's with the ball gown and the tiara?" I asked, for want of anything else to say.

"It's Hallo*ween*," she said. "I'm a *fairy*." She produced a magic wand and jabbed it at my face.

Hah! Not a chance—*she* was never one of the fay.

"Halloween isn't until tomorrow," I said, and went back to my magazine.

Unable to dispute the date, she was silent for a

DON'T YOU TRUST ME?

moment. "I can read," she said at last, apparently in a mistaken attempt to impress me.

"Good for you," I said. I shifted my position so as to minimize her view of my face.

A welcome silence followed this maneuver. Then—

"Juh-juh-jah-nell. 'Janelle'! That's your name, isn't it? See? It's on your boarding pass, right where *my* name is on mine."

"*What?*" I looked down at the little monster. She was holding up my boarding pass, comparing it with her own. "Give me that!" I snatched my pass—which had fallen on the floor—away from her. "Excuse me, ma'am," I said to the woman with the baby and small boy, "but could you call your daughter off, please?"

"Quit bothering the girl, Cee Cee," said the woman, without so much as glancing toward us. "Stop it, Jay Cee," she said, jerking irritably at the boy's suspenders. "Stop that right now. I mean it."

I gave up hope of deliverance from that direction and began looking around for another seat. The waiting room was filling up as the time to board approached, and there were few left. I did see one almost over into the next gate area. I stood up, happy to give the child the opportunity to torment someone else.

A man in a New York state trooper's uniform walked up to the desk by the gate entrance and began to speak with the agent stationed there.

I sat down again.

I buried my nose in my magazine. Various grinning airbrushed faces stared up at me from its pages. One star had been caught off guard and was grimacing hideously into the camera. DOES SHE NEED MORE WORK DONE? YOU BE THE JUDGE! shrieked the headline. Maybe she did need more "work" done, but what she really needed, I realized in a rush of actual, real empathy, was not to be followed around by cameras. I wondered how the photographer would look if somebody shone a bright light in his eyes as he was climbing out of a limo. *Stardom sucks,* I thought, and patted myself on the back for this Mother Teresa–like thought.

The trooper and the gate agent were surveying the crowd, the airline employee shrugging helplessly. She gestured at the entrance to the passenger boarding bridge.

Oho. They *were* looking for somebody, then, and she was suggesting that they'd catch the person as they presented their boarding pass. It was lucky I hadn't smarted off to this woman, like I had to the ticket agent, or she'd have remembered me for sure.

On the other hand, there was no reason to think that I was the person they were looking for. I mean, was I some kind of a bank robber or mass murderer who had to be stopped from fleeing the country? I was not. And who knew I was leaving? Brooke did, as she had seen my suitcase in the car's trunk, and I suppose that Janelle did, if Brooke had managed to pound that information into her teeny-tiny brain. How was either of those two going to tell anybody, much less guess under what name I'd be traveling? They weren't going to, that's how.

So, it wasn't me they were looking for. Still—

My eye fell upon Cee Cee, who was chewing on her boarding pass. Why were children so horrible?

"You know *my* name," I said, trying hard to sound amiable. "What's yours?"

"Cee Cee," she said. "Do you have a dog? I do."

"No, Cee Cee, I don't. Say, I have an idea." I bared my teeth at her. "Why don't we trade boarding passes? That would be kind of fun, wouldn't it?"

"No," she said briefly.

"Why not?"

"Because it's mine. It's got my name on it. Lookut." She poked at it with a fat finger. "It says 'Cee Cee' right there. You're not me. You're Janelle."

My temper, never very reliable when dealing with children, began to get the better of me. "Look, kid—"

"Flight eight two fifty-seven is about to begin boarding. Flight eight two fifty-seven nonstop to Richmond, Virginia. Please wait until your boarding group is called," the gate attendant said over the loudspeaker.

Should I make a break for it? No, the cop would be watching for that. How about if I sat tight until the plane boarded? He'd come and ask me if I was whoever it was that he wanted, and I would say no, I was waiting for a different flight, and then he'd say—

"Would a Miss Janelle Johanssen please come up to the desk at gate twelve C and speak with the agent on duty? Miss Janelle Johanssen."

Okay, it *was* me they wanted.

A relative silence fell over the crowd, although people were standing up and shuffling toward the gate entryway, pushing their carry-ons ahead of themselves. Cee Cee stared at me intently. She was obviously aware that they were calling me, and she was waiting for me to respond.

"Families with small children and infants, and passengers with disabilities, will be boarded first. All families with small children, and passengers with disabilities, please come to the gate entrance."

Well, thank goodness for small mercies. "Good-bye, Cee Cee," I said, smiling through gritted teeth. Her mother began collecting their various belongings. The baby began to scream again, and the line of passengers flinched, as though she was aiming an automatic weapon in their direction.

The cop was walking through the crowd, looking from face to face.

"Miss Janelle Johanssen," he said as he walked along. "Miss Janelle Johanssen, please."

"Hey, mister," piped up my wicked fairy godmother in piercing tones, reaching out to grab his sleeve. "Here she is. This is Janelle here."

She pointed her magic wand right at me.

21

"A KANGAROO FARM? YOU'RE JOKING, RIGHT?"
I demanded, staring from Brooke to Janelle and back
again.

"We were just little kids," said Janelle. She and
Brooke looked at each other and snickered.

When they'd first walked into the day room of the
juvenile detention center (they *said* it was a shelter,
but they wouldn't let us leave, so let's call a spade
a spade, shall we?) the two of them had been all
hushed and big-eyed, like they'd expected to witness
the listless inhabitants assaulting one another with
chainsaws, or injecting themselves with heroin in the
stairwells. After a few minutes of non-drama they'd
relaxed and started acting more normally.

The "shelter" was a house in the country a few miles from Albany, a tiny bit scruffy, surrounded by fields and low fences. It looked kind of like a horse farm, only without any horses. *Much* nicer than any accommodations I would have been offered in the same situation in LA, and I'd barely squeaked in by a hair. They offered short-term housing for kids under sixteen who'd run into not-too-serious trouble with the law. Janelle was sixteen, and so everybody was used to thinking of *me* as sixteen, which meant I wouldn't have been eligible. They figured out who I was without much difficulty, though, because my folks had reported me as missing. Even though the authorities had been looking in the wrong part of the country for me, it didn't take long before the descriptions matched up.

"Let me get this straight," I said. "Brooke, you're telling me that as a seven-year-old child, *you* wanted to raise kangaroos and slaughter them for meat?"

"No! Not for meat! Eew!" She stared at me like I was some kind of monster. Well, why else would you raise kangaroos? She seemed to realize this, as she gave a little shamefaced laugh. "I don't know. We wanted a farm with lots of kangaroos hopping around, and we swore a blood pact that when we were grown up, we'd really do it. Like Janelle said, we were just little kids. But you remember it, don't you, Janelle?"

"Like yesterday," she said, holding up her index finger

and smiling at her cousin. "Blood and spit together, they bind you for all eternity." Brooke smiled back at her and linked her index finger with Janelle's.

I rolled my eyes. A kanga*roo* farm had been my undoing. *That* was why she had gotten so suspicious and decided that I was not who I said I was. *That* was why she had come back home ahead of her parents, snooping around where she had no business. *And* told the new boyfriend, whose father was . . . you guessed it—the state trooper who picked me up at the airport.

Would you believe that those two girls found a sledge-hammer and managed to break a tiny little window in the basement and then crawl out of it? It was Brooke's doing, naturally. If it'd been Janelle on her own, she wouldn't have been discovered until the Luttrells went down there for their holiday decorations and found her skeleton propped in the corner festooned with spider-webs like a sinister Christmas tree. However, unfortunately Brooke *had been* there, and when I had gone to look for the suitcase, I could have seen the smashed glass all over the place if only I had used my eyes. By the time I was back at the airport looking at the departure board, the cops were already there, making inquiries about me.

When they caught up to me, all I had on my person was the ten thousand dollars in my money belt and a few hundred in my wallet. The immediate assumption was, *of course,* that I had stolen the money from somewhere, even though I *told* the trooper that I'd won it fair and square.

"It was the day of the racehorse benefit," I explained. "I met somebody there—a bookie, I guess he was—and I placed a bet on an outsider at the Breeders' Cup race. Actually, I placed several bets."

"What were the names of the horses?" the father of Brooke's boyfriend wanted to know.

"I don't remember all of them," I said, "only the one that paid out really big. Durn Tootin', that was the name of the outsider."

I was right, of course, and he'd find out soon enough when he checked. I *had* met a bookie that day—or stood next to him, anyway—and I'd heard him talking about the horse, and the upset in the race, resulting in his having to pay out a large sum to a single bettor.

My calm and cheerful manner was beginning to get the trooper down. We stared at each other for a moment in silence. He was actually kind of good-looking, I decided. Maybe Brooke's boyfriend would be too, once he'd gotten some meat on his bones. Of course, it could be that I was more attracted to older men than to adolescent boys. Teenage boys are too self-centered.

"What was the bookie's name?" the nice-looking trooper asked.

I widened my eyes. "I have no idea," I said. "I'd never made a bet on a horse before. I didn't know how it was done, but it seemed like it would be fun to try—especially since I'd been so involved in this charity for retired race-horses."

"So you handed over a wad of money to a strange man at a public event. Precisely how much did you wager, by the way?"

"Seventy-five dollars," I replied promptly, having heard this piece of information as well. "It wasn't as simple as that, though. I had to pick several horses to win or place—I don't remember exactly. It was com-plicated. But I was lucky." I smiled at him with girlish candor. "I'm kind of a risk-taker by nature, I guess, but I'm lucky, too."

"And where did the seventy-five dollars come from?"

"Oh, it was mine. My parents gave me some traveling cash."

He went on questioning me, but there was no proof that my story wasn't true. I was banking on my belief that Uncle Karl wouldn't want either Aunt Antonia *or* the IRS to know how much money he'd been betting in his poker games, and he would therefore not demand it back. So far, so good; I hadn't heard a peep out of him about his money.

That wasn't surprising, but the odd thing was, nobody had said anything about the suitcase full of money, jew-elry, and confidential documents. The other odd thing was that Brooke and Janelle had shown up here at the shelter to see me. They didn't seem that mad either. Oh, Janelle was a bit frosty, but not Brooke. They weren't much banged up, not from the fall down the stairs or from climbing out of the basement window. So I had been right: neither had suffered real damage as a result of my actions. Just a little friendly roughhousing— nothing to make a fuss over.

Brooke gave Janelle a significant look.

"Oh, right," Janelle said. She stood up. "Well, Morgan, it's been weird. I do want you to know that, whatever Brooke thinks, *I* think you're a real bad seed. So don't bother trying to contact me in the future. I know your name, I know what you look like, I know what your voice on the phone sounds like, and I know where your parents live. No calls, texts, e-mails, or in-person contact, 'kay? So, bye."

I smiled and inclined my head, graciously acknowledging her request. She was right; there was nothing more to be gained from pursuing *that* acquaintance. She picked up her purse and glared at me, annoyed that I remained cool and in control. A staff member walking through the room mistakenly decided to add a note of chummy cheer to the proceedings.

"Wow," gushed the female warder, "you three girls could be triplets—blond hair, blue eyes, everything. Are you sisters?"

"No, we're cousins," Brooke corrected her. Then she blushed. "I mean . . ."

Janelle pointed at Brooke. "*We're* cousins. That one"—
she pointed at me—"is our evil twin."

"*Janelle!*"

"Hey, you're welcome to your opinion, Brooke. That's
mine. I'll see you outside in a minute."

"Good-bye, Janelle," I said, my voice pleasant, even
though I was a bit annoyed that the staff member had
failed to notice that the two real cousins outweighed me
by twenty-five pounds apiece, *at least*.

I turned to look at Brooke. She was looking thoughtful, with a deep crease forming between her eyebrows. If
she didn't watch out, one of these days that crease wasn't
going to go away. I waited to hear whatever it was she
wanted to say to me in private.

She took a deep breath.

"I found the suitcase."

I nodded; I had guessed that.

"I put everything back."

"I see," I said, and thought about this information.
That meant that only Brooke knew the full extent of my
activities during my time in Albany. No wonder I had
heard nothing about the suitcase.

"It wasn't easy. I kind of had to guess about some of the
charities. There was just so much *money*," she said, her
eyes widening in wonder as she remembered the experience of disemboweling the suitcase. "It was *everywhere,*
in the pockets, in the zippered section, in the *lining*."

I nodded, also remembering. Yes, that suitcase had reminded me of a roast chicken à la Mrs. Barnes: stuffed to bursting with goodies, and then an herb butter applied under the skin to enrich the flavor. I sighed.

Brooke continued, the knot of concentration still creasing her brow, "If anybody questions the way I divvied it up, I'll take the blame. I'll say that you left the money with me and I got it mixed up."

"Why?" I asked.

"Do you mean why did I put it back, or why would I take the blame?"

"Either. Both." Once again I found myself staring at Brooke, totally mystified. Right when I thought I had normal, feeling, empathic humanity figured out, Brooke would do something that stumped me.

"Because—" She took another deep breath. "Because I don't understand you, and I really, really want to."

Well, that made two of us.

I shook my head, signaling noncomprehension.

"Oh, sorry. I'm explaining this wrong. It's hard to do, because it's kind of embarrassing."

I considered this. What did Brooke have to feel embarrassed about? I was never embarrassed, myself, so it was difficult for me to guess.

"I want to give you another chance. I want you not to have a felony conviction on your record. Did you know that stealing"—she actually reddened when she said the word "stealing," as if it were an obscenity—"anything over a thousand dollars is a felony? It's grand larceny. I looked it up." She regarded me with a long sorrowful gaze, as though I had just been diagnosed with terminal cancer.

Well, of course I knew it was a felony. People get *mad* when you take their money away from them. The more money you take, the madder they get.

"Why is that embarrassing?" I asked.

You may say, "Why should you care, Morgan, so long as she *does* give you another chance?" But I, too, wanted to understand. The more I understood about people like Brooke, the better prepared I would be in the future, assuming I ever ran into a weirdo like her again.

She blushed again and avoided my eye. "Oh, I don't know. It's like I'm setting myself up as judge and jury over you. I don't want you to think that I believe *I'm* perfect. Because I'm *not*," she said earnestly, as though I'd been arguing with her.

"I see," I lied. I did *not* see. She found herself in a position where her trust, and the trust of her family, had been violated. A guest in her home had lied, cheated, and stolen from her. She had done nothing wrong, but she felt embarrassed that *I* might be under the impression that she thought that *she* was perfect.

Furthermore, I had told her right to her face—well, okay, to the other side of a basement door—that I was one of the cold. I suppose she didn't understand what I meant by it. Besides, I think she needed to believe that, deep down, everyone is just like her.

Mentally I threw my hands up into the air in defeat. I would never understand Brooke.

But now what? What was the best way for me to behave at the moment?

I sighed. It was probably time for me to imitate pathetic Francea and blub about how sorry I was and how I would never do it again. But I did have to be careful. Brooke wasn't stupid. Or, yeah, sure, she was about some things, but not about everything.

The strange thing was, even though Janelle was a complete dodo, she was smarter in some ways than Brooke. Janelle knew me for what I was.

"Thank you, Brooke," I said, my eyes lowered. That seemed safe enough. Should I pretend not to know about the felony thing? No, better not.

"I got—I know I got crazy there," I said. "It was just—I don't know if you'll understand—but it was so *easy*." As I've said, when I lie, I tell as much truth as I can. And maybe I *did* get a little crazy. For *sure* it had been easy.

Brooke nodded sagely. "I guess your family—they're, well, they're not super well-off, are they? I mean—" She scrambled to retract this possible criticism. "Of course they're not *poor*, or anything . . ."

"Compared with the Styles family, they are," I said. Again, nothing but the truth.

"Yes, and I could see that you liked nice things. It's easy for me. I could pretty much have anything I wanted, so far as clothes and stuff goes, but I'm not interested. I can understand that that might be kind of annoying."

Yep, very true. I said nothing, but stared at my hands in my lap.

"And it's obvious that you are incredibly smart and talented. It seems so awful to have your potential blighted that way. Mom and Dad and Grandma feel that way too. Well . . ." She paused, doubtful for a moment. "Daddy not quite so much, I guess. For some reason Daddy is madder than the rest of us. It's odd, because usually he's not—well, not sensitive that way, like Mom and I are."

Ha. I hid a smile. I knew why Uncle Karl was so ticked off. Not only was I walking off with the lion's share of his poker money, but the rest of it had been inadvertently donated to various charities.

"Oh! And um . . . and this is really embarrassing, but I kind of have to ask . . ."

Now what was embarrassing Brooke?

"Did you, uh, find a super-big diamond ring in Mrs. Barnes's drawer? Because I assumed it was Mom's, but mom noticed it in with her jewelry and said it wasn't hers. And I'm afraid that Mrs. Barnes thinks the ring getting in with my mother's things had something to do with you, so she's kind of mad too."

I nodded.

"She—she says that she always kind of wondered about you. I feel terrible that it never occurred to me that it might be her ring. Well, I'm sorry I screwed up. I don't pay much attention to jewelry."

I was about to say "That's all right" but realized in time that it wouldn't be appropriate.

It was funny. Aunt Antonia might have been expected, given her job, to have guessed what I was, yet even with her inside knowledge she hadn't spotted me. But it turned out that Mrs. Barnes, a cook and housekeeper, had been keeping a wary eye on me. A sudden image of a little blue car running a red light as I drove away in Uncle Karl's Corvette flashed across my mind. I suppose she'd spotted me behind the wheel and wanted to know what was up. Well, well, what a cunning creature Mrs. Barnes was turning out to be!

Some response was required. "Thank you for everything, Brooke. I'm very grateful," I said in subdued tones. To a certain extent I actually was. If only she'd minded her own business . . . but no, that was water over the dam or under the bridge or whatever. The fact was that she'd caught me but was letting me off pretty lightly. So yes, I was grateful. Sort of.

"—but whatever you were thinking of, taking photocopies of those papers—stuff from the school, Mom's notes, Daddy's business records, I *don't* know," Brooke was saying. Well, of course she didn't know. She didn't have my imagination or my breadth of vision. "What was that about, anyway?"

I looked down again. "Like I said, I got pretty crazy there," I murmured.

"I guess *so*. They all looked like copies, so I shredded them instead of trying to put them back."

She took another deep breath.

"Anyway, I wanted to tell you. Mom and I talked to the judge who is hearing your case, and we pretty much know what's going to happen next. You'll be released into the custody of your parents—"

Ugh! I made a face.

"Oh, I was afraid of that!" Brooke was all remorse. I was rather touched. How did *she* know what a bore it was going to be for me to wind up back in that miserable little house in LA?

"I *told* Mom that when you said that stuff about your parents—I mean, Janelle's parents—shutting you up in your room and not giving you anything to eat, you were actually talking about your own parents. You were, weren't you?"

Once again I escaped catastrophe. Instead of glomming on to this story and riding it until it was dead, I hesitated. Then I said slowly, "Well . . . I might have exaggerated a little bit. But . . . yeah, basically."

"I knew it! We told the judge that, and she said there

would be a social worker coming around on a regular basis. So if they do *anything*, you have to promise me you'll tell the social worker. You will, won't you?" She leaned forward anxiously.

"I guess," I said. Inspired, I added, "But it's hard to turn in your own parents that way."

"Wow, it must be. But there won't just be the social worker looking out for you. The judge says you'll be subject to, um . . . court-mandated therapy. But see, that's good! It will mean somebody to talk to, somebody who can help you figure your life out and where you want to go from here. Don't you think that will help?"

I was silent for a long moment. Then I raised my eyes to hers.

"You know, I think maybe it will. But you know what would help even more? . . . I hate to ask this but . . ."

"What, Morgan?" she asked gently.

"I know Janelle doesn't want to hear from me ever again, and I don't blame her." Very wise of her. I wouldn't want to hear from me again either. "But would you mind if I wrote to *you* sometimes? You wouldn't have to answer or anything. It would be nice to think of you being out here, and to remember the time I spent with your family."

"Oh, Morgan, of course I'll write you back! We'll be e-mail pen pals. You'll see; we won't lose touch at all!"

"Thank you, Brooke," I said. "That means a lot to me."

I doubt she noticed until much later the loss of the gold-and-turquoise ring (a gift from the trooper's son, maybe) that I hooked out of her purse. It was really careless of her to just stuff it into her bag loose like that. I suppose she was going to get it resized. When she did notice, she was sure to blame herself, and rightfully so.

The trooper's son had good taste. It was a beautiful ring, and it fit *my* hand perfectly.

AND AFTERWARD . . .

I've been back in LA for nearly a month now. It's not as bad as I'd expected. I've grown and learned so much this fall, and people can sense it. They respond to me differently than they did before I went away. I have a lot more confidence and worldly wisdom. The kids at school look at me in a whole new light; I am working my way into the popular crowd since I've returned. And my parents are no problem. They watch me like a pair of mice watching the comings and goings of a large cat. I try to go easy on them, since they *are* providing me with food and shelter, such as it is.

But oh, my dear, *dear* Mrs. Barnes! How I miss you! I *am* sorry you think badly of me. And my horseback riding lessons and my private bathroom! Oh well. No sense in sighing for lost pleasures. At least I skipped winter in New York, which I hear is the pits.

Brooke and I text and e-mail back and forth quite often. It is harder for me to exercise my magic on her when I am not actually present, and sometimes I get the uneasy sense that she is a bit more aware of my manipulations than I'd believed. But the experience of writing to her is excellent training, as I am becoming more eloquent using the spoken word. Sadly, Brooke is quite intelligent in some ways, so I have to remember to be cautious with her. Still, it is a learning process for me, and good practice.

I plan to send the family a Christmas card, and perhaps another one to Grandma. After a few months I will send an e-mail to Aunt Antonia (note to self: Do not call her "Aunt Antonia" when I write), just to stay in touch. Uncle Karl is going to be the hardest nut to crack, but if I persist, I have no doubt I will eventually prevail. He always admired my spirit. He'll come around in time. A few successful poker games to make back the money he lost, and we'll be friends again. Besides, even though Brooke shredded those pages about his alternate accounting practices, I still know they exist, which could come in handy at some future date.

I am *loving* my therapy sessions! If only I had realized how helpful they would be, I would never have resisted being sent away to New Beginnings in the first place. I have no doubt that New Beginnings would have had hot-and-cold-running therapy on offer twenty-four hours a day, and I might have found it almost as valuable as my trip to upstate New York. It is *so* useful having some-one to teach you about basic human emotions, as well as helping you to develop strategies for getting along with others and making them like you. I am learning a lot.

In fact, I have begun to think of a new career instead of the law or not-for-profit management.

The charity scam is always nice to know, and will no doubt come in handy at various times during my life. If I want to splurge on a nice vacation, say, and haven't got the money, I can always fall back on it. But once you have a record of any kind, everything gets harder, or so I am told. So I have to indulge in illegalities only occasionally.

I think I would make a great psychologist, or even a psychiatrist. Yes, I know it's expensive to qualify, but what if I can convince the Styles family that I am a worthy cause? They could contribute to my education, couldn't they?

And having the kind of past I now own is not necessarily a negative in becoming a professional in the mental health industry. My therapist had a tough childhood, at least in her own estimation. Tough childhoods can lead to scholarships in that field.

I believe I could offer a whole new perspective on psychiatry.

Anyway, it's something to consider. My future is going to be dazzling—trust me.